FLIPPING NUMBERS

A novel

ERNEST MORRIS

Good2Go Publishing

Copyright © 2014 by Good 2 Go Publishing

This novel is a work of fiction. All the characters, organizations, establishments, and events portrayed in this novel are either product of the author's imagination or are fiction.

Published by:
GOOD2GO PUBLISHING
7311 W. Glass Lane
Laveen, AZ 85339
www.good2gopublishing.com
Twitter @good2gobooks
G2G@good2gopublishing.com
Facebook.com/good2gopublishing
ThirdLane Marketing: Brian James
Brian@good2gopublishing.com

Cover Design: Davida Baldwin
ISBN: 978-0990869405

Acknowledgments

First and foremost, I would like to thank God for blessing me with this gift. Without you by my side, I would not have been able to make it through the many roadblocks and burdens that were placed against me. It is because of you that I have stayed strong and focused.

I would also like to thank Mr. and Mrs. Michael Lopez. You believed in me and stayed true and loyal, even when I doubted myself. Thank you both! That really meant a lot to me.

I dedicate this book to my late mother Jacqueline Morris and my late aunt Cathrine Heckstall. Even though you are gone, you continue to give me the strength that I need to make it in this cruel world.

To my children, Le`shea Burrell, Demina Johnson, Sa`meer and Shayana Morris, you loved me through all my wrong doings and never gave up on me, even when I left you alone in a corrupt world full of vultures, with just your mothers to guide you. Everything I do now is for you.

I would also like to thank and dedicate this book to a host of important people in my life, none more important than Yahnise Harmon. Through my whole incarnation, you have never left my side. Yahnise no matter what happens in my life; you will always have a place in my heart. To everybody else Dwunna, Kimyetta, Lyric, Jamie, Sedric, Kevin, Theresa, Loveana, Maurice, Rasheed, Frank, Rhonda, Lisa, Nyia, Chris, Nakisha, Brandi, Zarina, Tasha, Bo, Dee, Tysheeka, Barry, Laneek, Donnie, Dave, Tyreek, Scrap, Alisha, Tamara, Ed, etc…the list goes on and on. If I didn't mention you, I apologize.

Thank you everyone for supporting me.

PROLOGUE

EJ sat at home in his basement office, talking to his best friend and partner about their come-up in the game. They had been best friends since high school and had never let anything or anyone come in between them. If you messed with one, you better be aware because the other one wouldn't be far behind. EJ was the total opposite of Ed. He was a friendly and outspoken person. EJ stood at 5'9, medium build, low haircut, weighing approximately 175 pounds, firm and cut up with a beard. He was the mastermind of his small organization. He could talk anybody into doing whatever he asked. He wasn't a violent person, but he could get that way if you forced his hand.

Ed on the other hand, was a cold blooded killer. He was a little thin, but stood at 6'5. His skin was a brown complexion and wore long braids. He was missing a front tooth from being hit with a bat when he was fifteen years old. He was one of the most ruthless people someone would never wanted to meet. Anyone who crossed EJ or Ed might as well tell their mother to get out her black dress. There would sure be a lot of slow singing and flower bringing once it was all said and done.

Even though they both had wives at home, they didn't hesitate to snatch up a little piece of pussy from time to time at one of the clubs they frequented on the weekends.

Right now though, they were in EJ's southwest Philly home and they were all about business.

"Damn dawg; we finally did it," Ed said while pouring himself a drink from the bar. He was overly excited about the chain of events that had taken place over the last year. "You said that we would be millionaires by the time we turned thirty and now look at us. We hit the million mark and we are only twenty-two. I didn't think it would happen to us this fast in the game, but you had a vision and we turned it into a successful enterprise!"

EJ sat in his desk chair with a cool smirk on his face, admiring what his best friend was saying. Just thirty minutes ago, they both had pulled up their overseas bank accounts and realized that they had reached the millionaire mark.

Although that mark came at a deadly and hefty price, it was well worth it. Neither of them thought that they would ever see so many zeros at one time in their accounts so soon. They were living the lifestyle of the rich and famous and to them; they were finally on top of the world.

"Yeah dawg, we have come a long way from living in the projects, playing with carts and shit, dry humping on girls, and pretending that we were driving cars. Now we are actually doing that shit, from driving luxury cars to fucking some of the baddest bitches. We are also living in some exotic ass houses," EJ said while looking at a picture of him and his wife Yahnise and their son Ziaire.

EJ met Yahnise in high school and back then, she never would have given him the time of day. She was one of the baddest girls in their school. With a caramel complexion, she weighed 135 pounds, very petite, with a nice ass, and just enough titties to hold in both hands. After EJ started getting money, she noticed the change in him. Now, five years later, they had been married for two of those years. Yahnise still had that same body, but her chest and ass were slightly bigger from giving birth to their one and a half year old son Ziaire.

EJ put the picture down, got up, and walked over to the bar where Ed was standing. He looked at Ed with a serious face and said, "We have to find out who this mole in our organization is and eliminate him or her immediately! We can never enjoy all of this wealth until that's taken care of. We were lucky to make it this far and now we have to be even more cautious."

"I know what you are saying and I have people working around the clock to find out what the fuck is going on. When they tell me something, I won't hesitate to put a bullet right between their eyes," Ed said while taking his 40 caliber out of his shoulder holster and cocking it back. "But for now, I have to get home before Tamara tries to kill a nigga." Ed walked towards the steps with EJ walking behind him.

They both knew that business was now over for the night. Their wives had not seen them in a week and it was time to get some much needed rest. Tomorrow everyone would be going to Ed's mothers surprise birthday party. What they didn't know was that it could be the last day of their freedom....

Chapter 1

Beep! Beep! Beep! The alarm clock went off letting EJ know that it was time to get up for school. It was his senior year of high school, all he had to do was get through this year, and he would be done with school for good.

Beep! Beep! Beep! It kept going off until he couldn't take the sound any longer. He jumped out of bed and turned the alarm clock off. He went into the bathroom to brush his teeth and take a quick shower. Twenty-five minutes later he was done and eating a bowl of *Frosted Flakes* waiting for his friend Ed to come pick him up for school.

EJ's aunt came downstairs to prepare for her first customer of the day, when she noticed him at the kitchen table. "Hey baby, why haven't you left for school yet?" she asked as she made herself a cup of coffee.

"I'm just waiting for Ed to get here. He should be here in a couple of minutes. You know he's never on time for anything," he said while getting up and rinsing out his bowl.

"You know this is your last year of school. Have you thought about what you're going to do when it's over? I refuse to see you out in those streets selling drugs and shit." His aunt looked at him waiting for a response that never came. Ever since his mom died when he was fourteen, she had been his legal guardian. His aunt owned a hair salon that was attached to her house and she was busy with clients on the weekends. She always gave him spending money, but it was never enough to do what he wanted. The drug game was tempting, but he didn't know the first thing about it so he had to get a little job in the airport at this pretzel shop called Aunt Anne's. He made about $300.00 every two weeks and that kind of helped him out with his clothes and spending money.

"I really don't know what I'm going to do yet Aunt Cat, but it won't be selling no drugs so you don't have to worry about that," he said as he grabbed his jacket hoping that Ed would hurry up. He was tired of her always lecturing him about his goals.

The only thing that was on his seventeen year-old mind was girls and money. He was seeing a girl from the hood named Lisa that he only called when he wanted some pussy. Lisa was a real freak and she would let him do almost anything with her. EJ wanted more though in terms of women and life. He felt as though he was too old to be staying with his aunt and wanted to get out as soon as possible.

Just when his aunt was about to respond to what he said, he heard the sound of loud music, and knew it was coming from Ed's car. "I'll talk to you later Auntie," EJ said as he ran out the door and jumped in the car.

Ed had a Ford Thunderbird that his mom had given him when she purchased a new car for herself. It had a nice sound system that EJ had helped him install. They stole the system from Jerry's Corner over on Passyunk Avenue. It was easy because no one ever paid any attention to them and the man that worked there was too old to even notice. "What's up nigga," Ed said giving EJ a pound.

"What's up with you nigga," EJ said as he shut the door. "That's my shit right there. Turn it up and let these bitches start sweating us," he said as Ed turned up Jay-Z's *Hard Knock Life, Vol. 2* album.

They both went to Southern High School on Broad and Snyder Avenue. EJ was by far smarter than Ed was when it came to education, but Ed was certified street smart and also had a way with the ladies. Women would drop their panties for Ed in a heartbeat. I guess you could credit that to his long braids and the fact that he had over sixty tattoos on his body. Women love the bad boy look. Plus he had game and could talk any girl into giving him what he wanted. EJ was shy when it came to women. Don't get it twisted though, he got plenty of pussy, but could never pull the one that he truly wanted. He really wanted this girl by the name of Yahnise.

Yahnise was from down the bottom (West Philly). She lived on 43rd and Westminster. She had a supermodel body and men drooled over her when she passed. She seemed like she only fucked with ballers though. Anyone who wasn't getting money and couldn't buy her whatever she wanted, shouldn't waste their time speaking to her. I guess you could say that she was way out of EJ's league.

When Ed and EJ pulled up in the school parking lot, a crowd gathered across the street. People were shouting and cheering as two girls were ripping each other's clothes off and pulling out each other's hair. Ed threw the car in park and jumped out, leaving the door wide open. EJ didn't know what was going on so he got out the car and looked around. He was thinking that his partner wanted to see some titties.

As he stood there, he noticed why his boy ran like that. It was Ed's sister Erica fighting. Upon further observation, EJ noticed that she was being jumped. He took off across the street to help his peoples. The two girls had Erica on the ground stomping her out when Ed approached and pushed them off of her.

Then he saw one of the girls spit in Ed's face as he made his way through the crowd. Before he could stop him, Ed punched the girl dead in her face, knocking her out cold before hitting the ground. Sirens erupted and the crowd dispersed. EJ grabbed Ed and Erica and they all ran back to Ed's car and jumped in. As soon as they left, the cops pulled up.

Erica had a bloody nose and her shirt was ripped open. Her skirt was torn on the side and it rose up her legs as she sat with them wide open. EJ couldn't help but stare at her perky breast as she tried to cover up herself. He had never looked at her in that way, but he got an instant erection when he looked down and noticed that she didn't have on any panties covering her bald pussy lips. He quickly took off his shirt and gave it to her. "Put this on until we get somewhere to hide out," he said and then turned back around fighting temptation.

"Thank you EJ and I know you were staring at my pussy. Too bad you're like a brother to me or I might have let you get some," she whispered in his ear and began laughing.

Ed looked at Erica and said, "What the hell is so funny? You just got jumped and once again I had to save your ass." He really looked pissed off at Erica. "Now that bitch might try to press charges if those cops push her to do so."

"The cops are the least of our worries right now," EJ said looking in the passenger side mirror noticing a car was following them. "I think we are being followed by a bunch of niggas. I'm counting at least four in that little ass Cavalier. Ed are you strapped?" EJ asked as he became a little nervous.

"Naw, but let's just see what happens before we jump the gun and start speeding for nothing," Ed said as he kept his eyes glued to the rearview mirror.

As they pulled up to the light on 21st and Snyder, the car full of men pulled right up to the back of them. Then the passenger door opened and gunshots rang out.

Bloc! Bloc! Bloc! Bloc! Bloc! Bloc! Bloc!

"Go Ed! Get us the fuck out of here!" EJ yelled as he ducked in his seat. Ed hit the gas pedal and pushed the Thunderbird down Snyder Avenue dipping pass car after car. The Cavalier was no match for the horse power of the Ford.

Bloc! Bloc! Bloc! Bloc!, was all you heard as the back window shattered causing glass to land on Erica as she ducked down screaming.

Once they were able to get away, they hit the expressway. Ed slowed the car down to make sure the cops didn't pull them over. He asked, "Is everybody okay? Did you get hit anywhere?"

"No, I'm good. You okay back there Erica," EJ asked as he looked in the backseat at her getting up off of the floorboard.

"I'm good, but who the fuck was that shooting at us and where the fuck is y'all guns at?" Erica questioned while brushing glass out of her hair. She knew her brother always stayed strapped.

"I don't know, but I sure intend on finding out," Ed said as he headed for his house on 67th Paschall Avenue. The whole time he silently wondered, *"Why didn't he put his gun in the car last night?"* That mistake almost cost him and his family's lives. He thought to himself that he would never make that mistake again. Now someone has to pay for this with their lives.

CHAPTER 2

November 20, 2008

Months passed since the attempted murder of Ed, EJ, and Erica and finally Ed received the phone call that he had been waiting on. "What's up Ed? I got the word on why those niggas were letting off on y'all. That was Peedi's people and he said he wants his money or else someone is going to get laid down. I can't believe you would get involved with that nigga and you know how he gets down," Gene said as Ed listened while getting his dick sucked from Neicy, the neighborhood smut.

Peedi was one of the biggest drug suppliers in the United States. He had the whole East Coast on smash and had half of the West Coast on smash as well. Ed had been secretly dealing with him for a couple of months now without EJ even knowing it. He never flashed his money around because he knew that his best friend didn't want anything to do with drugs. He thought that if he built a small squad and made some major paper that he could persuade EJ to join him and be his partner.

He owed Peedi five thousand dollars from the last package he had given him. He was short a couple of thousand so he was avoiding Peedi until he got all of his money. Deep down inside, he knew that hit was meant for him, but he didn't want anyone else to know. Sooner or later, it was all going to come out, but until then, he wasn't saying anything.

Ed pushed Neicy up off of him and went into the other room so he could talk in private. "Fuck that nigga! He'll get his money in a couple of days. If he touches one person in my family, I'll touch ten in his! One thing I don't like is when someone tries to threaten me or my peoples!"

Ed knew how dangerous Peedi was. He had seen plenty of bodies on the news that was a result of Peedi's people, but he also was a dangerous man. At the age of seventeen, Ed also had a small body count that only his best friend knew about. To be honest, he wasn't scared of him. He just respected him so he was going to give him his money. He just had to do a couple of licks (robberies), give him his whole 5 G's and be done with him. Then he was going to find himself a new connect that he could try to manipulate.

"Hey, I need you to take me on one of your licks so that I can get his money and pay him. I really don't need this type of beef right now," Ed said pouring himself a shot of Hennessey from his mom's liquor cabinet.

"You know I got you this weekend after Thanksgiving. Everybody will be out shopping for Black Friday so there will be plenty of cars to choose from. We can easily make 5 G's and I will split it down the middle with you so you can pay your debt," Gene said.

"That's what's up, but I have to go now because I have Neicy in the other room and I'm trying to get some pussy before my mom gets off. You know she be bugging about these ho's," Ed said finishing off his shot of Hennessey.

"I feel you, but when are you going to tell EJ about the hit? You don't want him walking around out there and niggas pull up on him on some Rah-Rah shit!"

"He ain't no bitch and he can handle anything that comes his way, but I'm gonna put him down on some shit just to keep him out of harm's way," Ed said with a bit of irritation in his voice. He didn't like the fact that Gene was right. He did need to tell his boy about everything because if anything happened to him, all hell was going to break loose.

"Well nigga I'll call you when I'm ready to go on the route. Just make sure that you answer your phone because we have to be in and out," Gene said as hung up before Ed could respond.

"Damn! I hate when he does that," Ed thought to himself as he headed back in the living room where Neicy was sitting on the couch playing with her pussy.

"I had to start without you because you were taking too long," she said as she seductively licked the juices off of her fingers while looking at Ed who was grabbing his dick through his shorts.

"Well come over here and let me taste it," he said as he took off his shorts and boxers. When Neicy came over to him, he ripped her thong off and bent her over the chair. She spread her legs wide and lifted her ass up in the air while guiding his hand between her legs.

Ed teased her by rubbing his thick, sensitive head across her ass cheeks. It felt so good to her that it caused her labia to spasm, greedily reaching out for more.

"Don't you fucking play with me Ed! Put it in now!" Neicy demanded. He laughed at the sight of her making her ass clap against his dick begging for it. "Bitch shut up and take this," he said as his penetration jolted through her body like electricity.

She grabbed the back of the chair, clutching it tight. "That's it baby! Do me like that! It feels so good!"

She matched his moves, tightened her pussy around him, pumping her hips in a hard steady rhythm before he stiffened and growled. "Ahhhh shit! I'm coming!" Right before he did, Neicy's pussy spasmed and she came herself.

After they both got dressed, Neicy left so that Ed could take care of some business before he went to pick EJ up from school. He didn't go to school that day because he needed to figure out what he was going to do about Peedi. School would have only distracted him from the matter at hand.

When he pulled up to his crib, Neicy was walking past, wearing this short ass skirt that barely covered her ass and some leggings because it was a little chilly out today. He invited her in so that she could keep him company until he had to roll back out. Now it was time to get back to business. The only problem was, he hadn't figured out how he was going to approach Peedi.

CHAPTER 3

It was the last day of school before the Thanksgiving holiday and EJ was headed to his last class of the day. As he was about to enter the classroom, he spotted the most beautiful girl he had ever seen in his entire life walking towards the room.

Yahnise was sixteen, but very much out there for her age. She stood at about 5'2, caramel complexion, and long hair down her back with a smile that could light up any room with her pearly white teeth. She had on a pair of *Apple Bottom* jeans and a matching, tight fitting *Apple Bottom* shirt that sat just above her navel showing off her piercing. She wore a pair of *Jimmy Choo* stilettos that made her look like she stood about 5'7 and her jeans fit her ass like a glove.

EJ had always seen her in his computer class, but today it was something about her that made him really want her. He wasn't getting any money like the little drug dealers in his class, but he wasn't broke. He knew that Yahnise was high maintenance and only the ballers had a chance to talk to her. As she approached with two of her friends, he held the door open for them and spoke as they entered the classroom.

"Hey Yahnise, how are you doing today? EJ said as all of the girls stopped and looked at him as if he had just cursed at them.

"Do we know you?" One of the girls asked staring at him. When he didn't respond she continued, "Unless you can get our hair, nails, and feet done, or take us on a shopping spree, do not speak to us unless we speak to you." They all laughed and continued walking into the classroom to their seats.

EJ wanted to say something, but instead he found his seat and sat down waiting for the teacher to give them their assignment. One of his classmates heard what the girls said and he came over and sat down next to EJ.

EJ looked up and said, "What's up Chan? Why are you looking at me like that?"

Chan was from New York. He came to Philly with his mom and dad when he was fifteen. They opened up a dry cleaners on third and Organ Avenue. What people didn't know was, Chan was a computer genius and could hack into just about any system if you gave him enough time. Chan and EJ talked, but not that much so it kind of caught EJ off guard when he came over to him.

"I heard what Sonja said to you when they came in and that wasn't cool," Chan said while booting up his computer. "How would you like to make some real money so that no one can ever look down on you again?"

EJ looked at him with a skeptical look on his face, wondering what he was saying. "I have a job at the airport so unless you're going to give me a better job, then I'm good," he said thinking that he wanted him to sell drugs or work at the cleaners that his family owned.

"No, I'm serious man. I can put you on to something that would make you a lot of money in one month. All you have to do is be willing to really listen and pay close attention to what I show you."

Now Chan had EJ's attention and wanted to know more about what he was proposing. "What do I have to do?" EJ asked curious to what Chan was about to say.

"You're going to the club Friday night;right?" EJ nodded his head yes. "Well, I will be at the bank across the street from there. I help my cousin clean up on Friday nights. The bank manager stays there with us until we are done and then she takes us in her office to talk about some things." Chan really had EJ's full attention now because he was wondering where this conversation was going.

"We mentioned your name a couple of times to her letting her know that you are a very smart individual, and with your brains and my computer skills, we could do some real damage. The question is; are you willing to put in some serious time and effort on this. We are meeting Friday at 11:00 p.m. You can walk right over from the club, sit in on the meeting, and be back over there by midnight. I can't really explain it all to you right now, but I will fill you in at the meeting." EJ was curious at this point. "So are you in or out?"

EJ was curious as to what the hell was going on that at first he thought it was a trick, but looking in Chan's eyes and looking at the way he dressed with all of the expensive jewelry, he had already made his mind up for him.

He always thought that Chan got all of that expensive stuff from his parents, but now he thought different. This would also explain the car that he was driving. He had a 400 GS Lexus with Dayton's on it. EJ looked at Chan and said, "I'll be there at 11:00." That sealed the deal.

Chan and EJ sat in silence for the rest of the class. EJ looked over at Yahnise and he couldn't help but notice the way her pretty lips moved as she talked. He wondered what they would feel like wrapped around his dick. These thoughts alone caused him to get an instant erection. At that moment, he made up his mind that he was going to do whatever it took to get that girl. She was wife material, despite her gold digging ways and he was going to make her his.

He was brought back to the present at the sound of the bell. It was time to get up out of there. "I'll see you on Friday at 11:00," EJ said as he shook Chan's hand, rushing out of the classroom before Yahnise and her friends came out.

When he made it outside, he walked over to the McDonald's to grab something to eat. He got to the counter to place his order, and saw a familiar face. It was a girl named Denver from Southwest Philly. She was one of the best boosters in Philly. She could get anything that anyone needed for under half price. She looked at him and said, "Welcome to McDonald's. Can I please take your order?"

"Yeah, can I get a double cheeseburger, medium fries, and a medium strawberry milkshake and while you are at it Denver, let me get your phone number because I will be needing your services real soon," he said while handing her a ten dollar bill.

She looked at him curiously and asked, "Do I know you from somewhere?"

Denver was a redbone with a nice body and a nice shaped ass. She always wore some nice shit courtesy of her get money schemes and EJ wanted to use her to grab him some shit when he came up.

"I see you around whenever I'm down Southwest. My best friend is Ed and he messes with your sister Shannon on and off."

"Oh yeah... I have seen you before. I knew you looked familiar when you first came in. You go to Southern, right?"

"Yeah, but I'm kinda running a little late so can we hurry this up a little," he said checking the time on his cell phone. "You gonna give me your number, right? So I can hit you up for your services soon?"

"Yeah, I got you," she said as she handed him his food and gave him her number. EJ programmed it into his phone.

"I'll hit you up later," he told her as he headed for the door. As soon as he got outside, he saw Ed sitting in the car waiting at the corner listening to State Property's song, *Chain Gang*.

He jumped in the car and gave his homie a pound. "What's up nigga? Why it take you so long to get here?"

"Traffic, but seriously I have some shit to kick it with you about on the way to your job. I know who tried to hit us," Ed said with a real serious look on his face. EJ knew whenever his friend looked like that; then something was really eating at him. He sat there and listened as his friend told him everything from the beginning to the end.

"Damn nigga! You could have been told me this shit. You know I got your back no matter what. I could have helped you get that nigga his money."

"I know dawg. It's just that I know how you feel about that drug shit so I was trying to be discrete about it. I never meant to put you or my sister in harm's way." Ed looked like he wanted to cry, but the gangster side of him wouldn't allow it.

EJ looked over at him and said, "Man no matter what, we are in this shit together. We ride together, we die together."

"I got this all worked out though. Me and Gene are going to do a lick on Black Friday so I can get the money that I owe Peedi."

"Do you need me to roll with you?" EJ asked not even thinking about the prior arrangement that he had already made with Chan. His only concern was helping his best friend out and everything else could wait.

"No dawg. This is an easy lick. We will be in and out within minutes. You just take care of whatever it is you have to do."

EJ wanted to tell Ed all about his plans for that night, but he really didn't know what was going on at the meeting his damn self. What he did know was that he wasn't doing anything without his best friend in on it. He decided to go on with his plans and both of them were going to have a long talk afterwards.

"Okay, but remember I'm just a phone call away if you need me," EJ said as Ed pulled up to the airport where EJ worked. "I'll hit you up when I get off. I'll catch a ride home with my cousin so that way you won't have to come back up here. I'm going to come to your mom's crib tomorrow and check on you."

EJ jumped out of the car and headed in the airport to work. He didn't even look back at his friend. Truth be told, he hated the fact that Ed had gotten himself into this predicament, but he was damn sure going to have his back.

He knew that Ed was quick to pop a nigga if he had to, but he was still worried about him. He just had to get through these next few days because he was anxious to find out what Chan and his people had in store for him. He could see the dollar signs as he headed up the escalator to work.

"*EJ I hope you know what you're about to get yourself into. There's no turning back come Friday night,*" he said to himself as he entered *Auntie Anne's* to begin his shift.

What he didn't know, was once he went to that meeting, it would change his, and everybody associated with him, lives forever.

CHAPTER 4

Friday Night

It was 9:30 p.m. and EJ only had an hour and a half before he had the meeting that he hoped would change his life. He dressed in an *Armani* suit, compliments of Denver boosting it from down South Street earlier.

When his cell phone rang, he checked the name on the screen and saw that it was Chan. "Yo Chan, what's up my nigga?" EJ said while putting on his other shoe. "I was just about to head out the door and go to the club."

"Well I'm glad that I caught you," Chan said, clearly happy. "It's been a change of plans. She wants you to meet her at her crib in Upper Darby. I will be taking care of some other stuff with my cousin, but we will meet you there by 11:00 p.m. Do you have a way to get there or do you need me to come scoop you up before we head that way?"

"Naw; I can use my aunt's car because she went to bingo with some of her friends. What's the address?" EJ asked while throwing on his jacket and heading for the door.

After Chan gave him the address, EJ jumped in the car and left. He checked the time and saw that he still had an hour to get there. He decided to stop over at Lex Pizza on 45th and Lancaster Avenue to grab something to eat on his way. What he was wondering while he drove down Lancaster Avenue was, *why did they change the meeting spot and most importantly why is it at her house?*

He was hoping that everything went according to plan because if it didn't, and something happened to him, all hell was going to break loose. He texted his best friend the address in which he was headed, and told him that once he left, he would text him again.

For someone that didn't know them, it would have looked like a regular text message, but in all actuality, it was an unspoken code letting his friend know that *"If you don't hear from me, blow this address up with everything in it."*

EJ grabbed his food, and made his way to Upper Darby so that he could get this meeting over with and maybe still catch the club scene before the night was over.

Meanwhile in Southwest Philly

Ed was playing *NBA Live* in his bedroom. He had just gotten the text from EJ and was wondering who he was going to see in Upper Darby. Just as he was about to win the game, his phone rang, pulling his attention from the T.V. and causing him to mess up. It was Gene so he knew it was time to get this money.

"Yo, what's up?" Ed said putting his controller down to listen.

"Yeah baby boy, it's time to go to work. I'm sitting outside your crib in a Chevy Lumina mini-van."

"I'm not even gonna ask you where you got that from," Ed said shaking his head. "I'll be out there in a minute."

Ed grabbed his jacket, then felt under his pillow, grabbed his 40 caliber, and tucked it in his shoulder holster that he always wore. He then grabbed his Dutch and weed and left the house before his mom or sister stopped to ask him a question.

Ed jumped in the van, shook Gene's hand, and asked, "What mall are we going to hit up?"

"We're going to Springfield Mall since we're so close. There's a lot of rich white people up there, plus we will be close to the garage," Gene said as they pulled off to handle their business.

"Spark this up while I put on this *Mobb Deep* shit," Ed said as he passed Gene the filled blunt.

"That's what the fuck I'm talking about! We will definitely be on our shit by the time we get there. Don't roll the other one up until we are on our way back home and counting all that money we are about to make," Gene said as they hit the highway in route to the mall.

Thirty minutes later, they pulled up to Springfield Mall. They rode around the parking lot looking at the expensive cars. There were so many to choose from, but they wanted to get two of the most expensive ones and then come right back and grab two more. All together, they had to get four cars and in return, they would receive ten thousand dollars (five thousand a piece) for all four cars from YG, who ran a chop shop right off of 676 in Media Philadelphia.

Once they took the first two cars, one of YG's workers would give them a ride back to the mall where they would grab the other two. As long as everything went as planned, then they would be in-and-out in no time.

"Yo, look at that all black Jaguar right there and look what's next to it," Gene said as he turned down the music.

"That's the new 425i BMW and the rims on it are fucking crazy," Ed said, anxiously looking at the two cars.

"Okay now let's find two more and we'll get them first and come back for those two."

"Let's get them now because by the time we come back they may not be here and they are definitely worth 10G's by themselves," Ed said wanting to jump out of the van.

"Alright nigga, let's park this shit and get this money. Start wiping everything down that we touched so when the cops find this van, they won't be able to I.D. us," Gene said, while looking for a parking space.

After they finished wiping down the stolen van and taking anything out of it that belonged to them, they went to retrieve their meal tickets (the cars) for the night. With the mall being so crowded and the security being so tight, it looked like they wouldn't be able to complete it.

Just when they thought it was going to be a no go, an opportunity presented itself. There was commotion coming from inside the mall and security and the police rushed inside to take care of it.

"Let's go handle our business before it gets crazy out here," Gene said running toward the cars.

Ed ran behind his man and when they got to the cars, they each pulled out their jimmies and quickly opened the doors. Both of the cars had alarm systems that immediately went off. The two guys wasted no time deactivating the alarms and started the cars up. Once they both had their cars started, they hurried out of the parking lot to get to the shop undetected.

Twenty minutes later, they pulled up to an electric fence with a call button. Gene pushed the button and a few seconds later, the gate opened. The garage was in the back of an industrial warehouse, that one would only find if they knew it was there. That's how discreet YG was about his operation, as only a select few knew about it.

Ed followed Gene through the gate and headed for the opening garage door. As they rode pass, Ed couldn't help but admire all of the luxury cars that were parked in a line as if it was a car show. "*Damn, I got to get me one of those,*" he said to himself entering the garage and the doors shut.

Gene stepped out of his car first followed by Ed. Two men armed with machine guns approached the two, but didn't say a word. The back door opened up and YG and a skinny white guy walked out talking, ignoring Gene, Ed, and the two armed men.

"So I guess our business here is done then. It was nice meeting you and hopefully we will do some more business in the future," YG said to the white man as they shook hands.

The white man smiled and said, "There is no other person that I would rather do business with. Just make sure that my shipment arrives on time and we will be talking again in about a month or so."

The white guy then jumped in the backseat of his limo and the driver pulled off as the garage door started to open again. YG looked over at Gene and Ed and asked, "So what have you brought me this time?"

"These are two of the latest models that just came out. I don't think we will be able to snatch anything else tonight because it's too much security around. I'll try to go back out on the weekend," Gene said pointing to the cars.

YG walked over and inspected the cars as if he was a customer at a dealership. After a few minutes, he looked up and said, "I'll give you 6G's for both of them. That's three thousand a piece and not a penny more. Usually you would bring me four in one night, but since it's only two, this is a good deal."

Gene thought about it for a minute and realized that he was actually coming up an extra stack. He would get ten for four, but he was getting six for two because of the models he brought in. He looked over at Ed who nodded his head in agreement and then he looked at YG and said, "Deal."

They each walked out of there three thousand dollars richer. YG offered to give them a ride, but they wanted to take a cab home. They didn't feel like being bothered with his men after they acted as if they wanted to splatter their brains all over the place earlier. That was the first time since Gene had been dealing with YG that his men had pulled their guns out on him, but it likely wouldn't be the last.

CHAPTER 5

EJ arrived at the address that Chan had given him around 10:50. The meeting was scheduled to take place at 11:00 so he was a little early. As he pulled up to the address, he said to himself, "I can definitely see myself in a crib like this real soon."

He looked up at the immaculate mini mansion and couldn't believe his eyes. When he got to the door and rang the bell, a white man in a black suit opened the door.

"I'm here to see Maria," EJ said, glimpsing at the inside of the house.

"Name please," the white man said, while trying to block his entrance.

"My name is EJ and I'm a friend of Chan's. I was told to meet him here for a meeting at 11:00," he said while getting a little irritated.

The butler invited him in while he went to find his boss. When he came back, he escorted EJ to the back of the house where Maria's office was. "Knock before you enter," the butler said as he turned around and went back to the front of the house to finish doing his job.

"Knock! Knock! Knock!"

"Come in," a voice said from the other side of the door. EJ entered the office and saw a very attractive Spanish looking woman sitting behind a mammoth oak desk with a bunch of pictures on it.

"EJ it's finally good to meet you," Maria said as she slowly stood and walked from behind the desk. Once Maria was in EJ's full view, he studied her from head to toe. His eyes immediately locked when they saw her fat ass. The tight black spandex she wore didn't help the situation at all.

"I'm glad you could make it on such short notice," Maria said picking up a bottle of Hennessy from her desk and pouring herself a drink. "Would you like anything to drink?"

EJ shook his head no and said, "If there is money to be made then I'm all for it. I'm tired of only making enough money to get by week to week."

"Well stick with me and you won't have to worry about that ever again," she said walking back behind her desk and taking a seat.

"Okay, let's get straight down to business then," Maria said as she saw Chan and his cousin walk in. They shook EJ's hand and gave Maria a hug before pulling up a couple of chairs next to EJ, facing Maria.

"Basically I brought you here because I know we can help each other," she said, getting straight to the point.

"How you figure," EJ questioned getting up to take his *Armani* jacket off and placing it on the back of his chair before sitting back down.

"Simple. I want you to assist Chan in running an operation that I'm trying to set up. You will never have to worry about money again if you do this right and stick to the script," Maria said taking a sip of her drink.

"Damn! You are the answer to all of my problems," EJ chuckled. "I just have one request though. If you bring me in, then you have to bring in my best friend and partner. I don't do anything without him," EJ said with a serious look on his face.

Maria looked at Chan and his cousin Wan and they both nodded their heads yes. "So what is your friend's name?" Maria asked sipping her drink.

"His name is Ed and I trust him with my life so you don't have to worry about any backlash from his decisions."

"Good then. He will be your responsibility, not mine," Maria said as she stood and started towards the door. "Follow me guys."

They all stood up and followed Maria down the hall to another room. The whole time EJ's eyes were glued to Maria's ass as it jiggled with every step she took.

When they arrived at the room and walked in, it looked like a C.I.A. headquarters. You would have thought she owned a computer store with all the equipment in there. Everything was state of the art. You could make anything you wanted in there from I.D.s to your own T.V. show. EJ's head was spinning from being so excited.

"I'm glad you like what you see," Maria said turning to EJ, Chan, and Wan. "Get used to this place because you will be spending a lot of time in here preparing for the next phase of this operation."

She showed them around the room and when they were done she said, "Now let me explain to you what needs to be done."

"Have you ever read about or seen on the news anything about the banks losing a lot of money to people filing bogus insurance claims? Well what we are about to venture into is ten times better than that," she said as they all sat around a computer screen as she booted up the computer.

"I have over one hundred account numbers here that I downloaded from my computer at work. The date that we have here will help us set up one of the biggest bank scams in history," she said as she typed on the computer to print a list of the account numbers for everybody to glance over.

They looked over the papers that Maria had printed when she began to talk again. "All of you are very young and if y'all stick with me, you will be three rich young men."

"Uh don't you mean four rich young men," EJ said smirking at Maria.

"Yes. How could I forget about your partner? We all are partners now so get used to having five people around," she said while sitting on the edge of the desk. "When will I be able to meet your friend?"

"I can have him here first thing in the morning if you like," EJ said, while staring at Maria's pussy lips poking through the spandex tights. He had to turn his head to avoid being caught lusting after the older woman.

What he didn't know was that Maria was only twenty-two years old. She graduated from Germantown High School at the top of her class. She went to Temple College for three years and received a Bachelor's degree majoring in Computer Programming and minoring in Business Management. She began working at TD Bank a year ago and was already the manager of the branch.

She was focused on becoming the first young Spanish District Manager. Her goals were set until she stumbled onto a scheme that could help her move up even faster. She just needed someone who could design the checks and someone who was intelligent enough to create an enterprise worth taking that risk.

That's where Chan, EJ, and Wan came into play. Even though she didn't know much about Ed, she could tell by the way EJ spoke of him that he would be a reliable worker.

"That won't be necessary because I won't be up early in the morning," Maria said, taking another sip of her Hennessey. "I would like to fill y'all in on the whole operation, but I want everybody here at the same time."

"At least tell us what we will be doing," EJ said, waiting for a response.

Maria stood and began breaking it down for them. "Well first we will be printing up some checks and changing the last number of the account. We cannot go pass ten thousand dollars or the FEDs will be on to us. In time when we can establish a solid pattern, we may be able to go pass that point. What we need to find out is how much can we deposit at one time. I will work on that part even though I think I already know the answer to it," she said as she looked around the room, making sure everyone was with her.

"We will need some people to actually go into the bank and cash some checks. I will make sure that goes smoothly because I will be the one who will authorize the transaction. Are y'all with me so far?"

Everyone nodded yes and continued to listen as she explained what needed to be done with the rest of the plan.

"I will leave the recruiting up to y'all. I will never be seen when y'all are dealing with these people. Only the four of you will ever know about me. To everyone else, this is y'all operation. Are we clear on this?" Maria said with her face now serious.

"I'm going to stop here until we meet up here tomorrow at 5:00 p.m. Do not be late and be prepared to be here for a while. I know you want to go over to the club and enjoy yourself before it closes EJ so I will let you go. I already kept you here too long," Maria said looking at her watch and seeing that it was 1:00 a.m.

"I think I might pass on that tonight. I have to go catch up with Ed and make sure he is straight and focus on tomorrow," EJ said as he gave Maria a hug along with Chan and Wan. Maria walked them to the door and watched as they got into their cars and pulled away.

She was thinking to herself, "*I hope I'm making the right decision about these guys.*" She closed the door and went upstairs to her master bedroom suite to take a hot shower. Tomorrow was going to be a long day and she wanted to be well rested. It will be the beginning of a new partnership with a couple of hungry lions. She had a feeling that EJ would be the one to watch. He seemed calm and cool, but he also seemed like he could be the most dangerous one out of them all. In fact, she thought he was going to be the one who took this whole operation to a whole new level. She was sure going to find out.

CHAPTER 6

EJ arrived at Ed's crib at 2:00 a.m. He talked to him and told him that he was coming over. Ed told him that he would be in late because he had to drop the money off to Peedi. When he pulled up to the house, he didn't see Ed's car so he called Erica's phone.

RING! RING! RING!

"Hello," she said in a groggy voice waking up out of her sleep. Usually she would still be in the streets at this time.

"Sorry I woke you up big head, but are you in the house?" EJ said as he sat in the car finishing his *Dunkin Donuts* bagel.

"Yeah boy and what do you want at 2 in the morning," she said, checking the time on her phone.

"I'm outside. Come open the door for me. I have to wait for Ed and you know he probably won't be here for a couple of hours. Plus I don't feel like driving home tonight anyway," he said as he got out of the car.

"Okay. Here I come," Erica said, jumping out of the bed, heading down the stairs to let in EJ.

When she opened the door, she turned to go back to bed. EJ's eyes were glued to her ass. She was wearing a pair of booty shorts and a tank top. He never really looked at her like that, but ever since he had seen her bare pussy that day in the car and whispered in his ear, he wanted to hit that in the worst way.

"Where you going, big head? You have to stay up and keep me company for a while."

"Boy I'm going back to bed. You better come upstairs and watch T.V. in my room. You know the T.V. down here don't work," she said as she went back up the stairs.

Usually he would go in Ed's room and wait, but Ed had begun locking his door because Erica and his mom had been going in his room when he wasn't home, taking his stuff. He followed Erica up to her room so he could watch T.V.

Erica laid on the bed and pulled the covers over her while EJ sat at the end of the bed and grabbed the remote. When he turned on the T.V., *Monster Ball* with Halle Berry was on the channel.

"This is one of my favorite movies," he said, getting comfortable by kicking his shoes off and lying at the bottom of the bed.

"You just want to see her fuck Bob Thornton with your nasty ass," Erica said kicking him in the back playfully.

"Keep your ugly feet to yourself," EJ said as he swatted her feet away and grabbed his soda from the floor.

Erica sucked her teeth. "Ugly?" she echoed. "Nigga please! Ain't nothing ugly on my body," she said in a tone that was matter of fact.

"I know ugly when I see it," EJ nodded and finished his soda off and throwing the bottle in the trash can on the side of the bed.

"That's your word?" Erica asked pulling the covers off of her and jumped out of the bed walking around to the front where EJ was now sitting.

"Is this ugly too," she asked while turning around and shaking her ass in his face. EJ cleared his throat as he sat and watched her ass bounce. Then she turned around and laughed while her nipples were fighting to escape the tank top.

"Can I help you," he asked as he looked at her titties and then down to her pussy poking out under her boy shorts.

"I don't know. Can you?" Erica said as one of her eyebrows rose. Not being the type to back down from a challenge, EJ grabbed Erica and buried his face in her titties. Then he lifted her tank top over her head and took his time sucking on each one of her nipples.

"Damnnnn," Erica moaned and cursed as he grabbed his head and begged him not to stop. Two minutes later EJ picked her up and laid her on the bed. He then pulled off her boy shorts exposing her cleanly shaved pussy. She was already so wet that her juices were flowing out of her and dripping down her legs. EJ bent down and sucked on her clit, massaging it, and then he began eating away while fingering her at the same time. Erica couldn't take it any longer. He was forcing her to cum quicker than she anticipated. After that mind blowing orgasm, she had to save face.

"Stand your ass up," Erica demanded as she grabbed EJ's rock hard dick through his *Armani* pants. She unbuttoned and unzipped his pants and slid them down along with his boxers. He stepped out of them and took his shirt off.

Erica grabbed his dick with two hands and licked, sucked, and tongue kissed it. She made sure she slurped all of the saliva off of his dick before opening her mouth as wide as she could. She was only able to take in half of his dick before letting it slide back out of her mouth making a loud slurping sound. For the next five minutes, Erica sucked the shit out of EJ's dick. The whole time making loud noises until he finally exploded in her mouth. Without a second thought, she swallowed the mouthful of cum like a soldier.

"I see I still hold the dick sucking title," she said as she wiped her mouth with the back of her hand.

"I'm not finished with you," EJ said still hard. He wanted some of that pussy now. He grabbed Erica and laid her on the bed. Then he put her legs on his shoulders and entered her warm slippery walls.

"Oh shit Daddy! Tear that shit up!" Erica yelled as EJ pounded away at her pussy. Two minutes later, she was cumming again.

He turned her over, pulling her ass up in the air and entered her from behind. Her ass was bouncing up and down as he pumped every inch of his manhood into her.

"I can't take it no more! You are killing me!" Erica said trying to run from him, but he had a tight grip on her waist.

"Shut up! This is what you wanted so now I'm giving it to you," EJ said as sweat ran down his body and over Erica's ass cheeks.

Ten minutes later EJ couldn't hold it any longer so he pulled out and exploded all over her ass and back. They both laid on the bed for a couple of minutes before Erica got up and went to the bathroom. She came back out and brought EJ a warm soapy rag to wash up. Afterwards he dressed while Erica got back in the bed naked and laid under the covers.

"So what are we going to do about what just happened?" Erica questioned, watching EJ fix his clothes.

"I don't know, but we both know that we crossed the line and we can't do that anymore," EJ said looking at her. "Ed is my best friend I don't want that to change so let's just keep it at that. What happened here stays here!"

"Okay I can do that, but I will want some more of that Mandingo dick one day and you will give it to me," she said with a smile on her face.

EJ smirked and shook his head while getting up and heading downstairs to wait for Ed. He fell asleep on the couch waiting for his friend to get home. He knew he had crossed the line with Erica, but it was a line he didn't mind crossing. He didn't know if he would do it again.

* * * *

"Well I got the money that I owe you so now you can call the dogs off," Ed said as he sat across from Peedi at the I-Hop on Chestnut Street. It was 2:45 a.m. and Peedi had just left Club Transit when he received a call from Ed asking him to meet him there.

"You should have had my money and that shit wouldn't have never happened. Next time you'll come correct or don't come at all," Peedi said shoving a fork full of the blueberry pancakes in his mouth that he had ordered.

Peedi was real cocky, but Ed was trying to stay calm. Peedi only acted like that because he had three niggas with him that were packing submachine guns. Little did Peedi know, one day soon, Ed would try to get him for attempting to hit him and his family.

"Well I guess our business here is done," Ed said getting up from the table to leave.

"Our business is never over. In fact, I put something in your car for you. Just bring me the same thing back as before," Peedi said, continuing to eat his food, never looking up at Ed.

"I don't think you heard me correct," Ed said sitting back down at the table. "I'm done with that shit and our business relationship is over. I have something different lined up so you can take whatever it is you put in my car out and I will be leaving."

One of Peedi's men stood behind Ed. He noticed alertly, but he didn't make a move because he was outnumbered.

"I know you got yourself a new connect out in Jersey and I respect that, but we had a formal agreement and I know you are not going to break that. Are you?"

"My other connect has nothing to do with you and our agreement was never an agreement. Now unless you are willing to start something in front of all these people, I'll be leaving and I will sit your merchandise on the ground for one of your toy soldiers to pick up on your way out," Ed said, getting up and headed for the door without looking back at the two goons following him. He had already unsnapped the 40 Caliber out of his shoulder holster and discreetly put it in his jacket pocket.

When he got outside, he headed for his car taking quick steps. The two goons also picked up their pace. When he reached the part of the parking lot where his car was, he took out his car keys with his left hand while he slipped his 40 Caliber out of his jacket with his right.

The two goons both reached inside their jackets for their weapons, but it was too late. Ed spun around in one quick motion and fired off four shots hitting both of his targets in the chest.

All one could hear was BOOM! BOOM! BOOM! BOOM! Then all the people in the parking lot began yelling and running. The two goons were dead before they hit the ground.

Ed jumped in his car, pulled out of the parking lot, and quickly drove around the corner. He knew with what had just happened; things with Peedi would never be over until he was dealt with.

"Let's get out of here," Peedi said as he and one of his goons rushed out the door. They ran to Peedi's Range Rover and jumped inside, but before they could even pull away, Ed was standing on the driver's side of the truck.

BOOM! BOOM! BOOM! BOOM! BOOM! That was all that was heard as the driver's head exploded and chest was ripped open.

Ed then walked over and opened up the passenger door. "What do you want man? If it's money, I have a couple thousand right here. Take it and I will not try to retaliate," Peedi said taking the money out of his pocket passing it to Ed in a plea for his life.

Ed took the money and said, "It wasn't about the money. If I had left, you would have had a contract out on me by the morning. So I guess I can sleep well tonight while you sleep good forever," he said while putting two bullets right between Peedi's eyes. BOOM! BOOM!

Ed rushed back to his car and took off before the cops showed. He reached into his back seat and pulled out the bag. When he looked in the bag, a large eighth of raw was inside, and now he had it all to himself. He smiled as he headed home.

CHAPTER 7

When EJ woke up the next morning, he could smell the aroma of bacon and eggs being cooked. His stomach growled from the smell, and sat up, put on his shoes, and walked to the kitchen.

"Good morning sleepy head. What time did you come here last night?" Ed's mom, Ms. Cynthia, asked.

Ms. Cynthia was a beautiful woman and at the age of thirty-five, she still looked like she was twenty-one. She had brown skin with long black natural hair. She was 5'7" with a flat stomach that looked like she never had two kids. Her ass was a perfect bubble. I guess you could tell where Erica got her body from because she was flawless from head to toe.

"I came in this morning at like three looking for Ed. Did he come in yet?" EJ asked while looking in the refrigerator for something to drink.

"Yeah, that fool is upstairs sleep. Go get him and Erica and tell them to come eat because I'm about to leave for work," Ms. Cynthia said as she grabbed her uniform jacket. "You can stay and eat before you leave. It's plenty for all three of y'all. I will see you later," she said as EJ gave her a hug and kiss on her cheek.

Ms. Cynthia worked at Philadelphia Parking Authority (PPA) where EJ's mom previously worked before she died. She was the shift supervisor so all she did was drive around, checking on her workers.

"Alright, you be careful out there," EJ said as he ran upstairs to get Ed up. They had a lot of shit to talk about before they went to the meeting at five.

When EJ got to Ed's room, he was already awake and hiding something under his mattress. "What's up nigga? I've been waiting for you all night. Where the fuck was you at; fucking one of your little ho's," EJ said sitting on the chair in Ed's room.

"Naw, I had some problems last night when I met up with Peedi," Ed said, looking incredibly nervous.

"What happened and why didn't you call me? You know I would have been there ASAP!" EJ said, watching his friend pacing back and forth.

"It's a long story and we will talk about that later. Right now, I want to know what's up with you. In your text, you said you have some big plans for us. I'm all ears my nigga so start talking," Ed said sitting on his bed ready to spark a Dutch that he had rolled a few minutes ago.

EJ got up and walked towards the door. "We'll talk at my house. I have to get Aunt Cat her car back so come on and follow me to the crib."

"Alright go ahead. I'll meet you there in a half hour. I'm going to freshen up a little," Ed said heading for the bathroom.

"Don't be late nigga. This is some serious business," EJ said leaving to return his aunt's car.

* * * *

When Ed arrived at EJ's house, they sat down and talked for over two hours. First EJ explained everything to Ed that Maria had told him about the operation. Then Ed told him about what happened the previous night at the I-Hop.

"So did anyone see you roll out? Cause if they did, you have to get rid of your ride," EJ said concerned for his friend.

"No, I was out of there before the cops even came, but I like this scam that y'all are planning and you can count me in," Ed said, as he fixed himself a drink at the bar.

"Okay, we have about four hours before our meeting so I might as well kick your ass in some Madden," EJ said, setting up the game. "And don't forget to get rid of that burner also."

"Yeah, I'll take care of it tonight after the meeting," Ed said as he sat next to his friend to Madden.

* * * *

At 5:00 p.m., everybody was sitting around the table at Maria's house; Chan, Wan, EJ, Ed, and Maria. Maria looked like a gangster with her army fatigue pants on and a white wife beater. She had on a pair of black Timberland boots and her hair was tied in a neat bun on top of her head. Everyone was sipping on a glass of Remy except for EJ who was drinking Pepsi. They were all waiting patiently for Maria to begin the meeting.

"Well now that we are all here, let our first official meeting begin," Maria said as she sat her drink down and stood up. "First and foremost it's nice to finally meet you Ed. I've heard a lot about you."

Ed looked at EJ and then at Maria. "I hope it wasn't all bad," he said with a grin.

"No, it was nothing but good things. Now let's get back to business," she said seriously. "As I was saying the other day, we are going to take this city and every other city by storm. I have over one hundred account numbers to start with. We are going to print off a few as a test run and see how authentic they look. What we will need is someone who is not scared to walk up in the bank and try to cash it," Maria said looking around the room.

"I'll do it," EJ said volunteering for the task. "I think we should try it at another bank instead of yours first. If anything goes wrong, it won't set off any red flags there and then we can still come back to your bank and do it there as planned," he said waiting for Maria's response.

"That's why you are the brains of this operation," Maria said in agreement, to what EJ had said. "Are you sure that you are comfortable with going in there like that? What if something goes wrong?"

"That's just it. If something goes wrong or even looks like it's about to go wrong then I will walk away and get out of there as fast as possible," EJ said, taking a sip of his soda.

"Alright then, let's get this thing started gentlemen. Let's get to the computer lab," Maria said as she headed out of her office with everyone following behind her.

* * * *

Everyone was seated at a computer monitor as Maria booted up the system. Once it was up and running, she punched in the banks access code and over one hundred, customers' account information popped up.

"How did you transfer everything to this computer?" Ed asked in amazement.

"I used a flash drive and if you are not familiar with that, I'll show you at another time," Maria said as she walked over to one of the pictures and removed it from the wall and showing the safe behind it. She hit the pad with the combination numbers and it popped open. She took out a pack of paper and brought it over so that everyone could see it. "This is called watermark check paper. Without this, you cannot make a check. Regular paper will get you locked up before you can even collect the money," Maria said with a serious face.

"EJ and Chan will be in charge of creating the checks. They will then pass them off to Wan and Ed so that y'all can distribute them to the squad that each of you will hire. I wouldn't get any more than six people to start off with at first."

"I was thinking of only four outsiders and Wan and Ed," EJ said to

Maria. "That way it will only be four people that are not in our immediate circle. Once we gain their trust then we can expand and make this into an empire. Does everyone agree with that?" he said watching everyone nod their heads.

"While Chan and I design the checks, I want the rest of y'all to be going through the phone books and picking bank branches outside of the city. We will never cash a check in Philly unless it is at Maria's bank and she is there to approve it," EJ said as if he was the boss.

In his mind, this was going to be his organization. He felt as though he knew how to operate it better than Maria did. Maria was teaching him too much too fast and it wouldn't be long before he wouldn't didn't need her help any longer.

CHAPTER 8

Around 9:00 p.m., EJ and Chan had designed four different types of payroll checks. They used PECO Energy, Jack's Catering, Septa Transportation, and The Eagles Organization. In total, they had over $5,500.00 worth of checks as a test run. If everything ran smoothly then they would up the amount and begin making major doe.

Wan and Ed had located twelve different banks to choose from outside of the city. They had two locations in Upper Darby, three in Lower Merion, three in Chester, and four in New Jersey. Now the only thing was they had to wait until Monday to pull this off. They had already planned on leaving school early so that they could hit the banks before they closed.

EJ decided that he was going to test the waters by attempting to cash the Eagles payroll check. "On every check it has a phone number just in case the bank tries to call the company. The numbers are linked to Maria's pre-paid cell phone. She already knows what to do if she gets a call from them. Chan will explain this a little more," EJ said as he looked at Chan.

"I've made each check with an encrypted sequence of numbers. They match the real account numbers to the tee. The only difference is the last number. Once they enter the real routing number and account number, it will come up as if it's correct. Once they cash the check, the original account numbers will be placed back into the banks computer as if it never changed. I will be here making sure that it all goes well. If I have any problems, I will text "abort," and that means don't go in or leave ASAP," Chan said making sure everyone knew the severity of what he was saying.

"EJ is going to be the first one to test this so that means everyone else will be on standby. If it's a go, he will text everybody else to proceed. You will be in groups of two. One person will go in and cash the check while the other person will be the look out. Any sign of danger what so ever, get out of there immediately! Even if you have to leave your ID and the check. We will worry about that later," Chan said as he showed everyone the printed work.

Maria was amazed at how authentic the checks looked. Chan and EJ had really created a masterpiece. "EJ and Ed will go together on this one and Chan and Wan will be on standby. Chan will show me what to do here on the computer and I will access the numbers. Are we all clear on this," Maria said as they all nodded in agreement.

"Okay, this meeting is adjourned until Monday. Enjoy the rest of your weekend and we will meet back up at 12:30. That should give all of you plenty of time to go to school, get all of your work, and leave early. Take care and be safe," Maria said as she walked everybody to the door.

"See you guys later and try to stay out of trouble," Maria said as she shut the door behind them.

"Let's go out to the club and celebrate," EJ said to Ed and Chan as they were about to get in the car.

"Well, Wan and I have to take our girls out tonight. We promised them that we would after the meeting. Maybe next time though," Chan said shaking EJ and Ed's hands before getting in the car and pulling off.

"Well I guess it's just us tonight my nigga," Ed said, getting in the car and unlocking the door for EJ.

EJ shut the door and leaned back in the seat. "Yeah so let's go party and have some fun. Let's go to the "Set It Off" over on 2nd and Cambria and see some bitches shaking their ass," he said putting on his favorite rapper Jay Z's, The Dynasty Album.

"That's what the fuck I'm talking about," Ed said as he pulled off, heading for the strip club. EJ and Ed had not enjoyed themselves all week so now it was time to unwind.

* * * *

On Monday, everyone was in school as planned. They attended all of their classes except the last one. Ed was the only one who had eight periods. Everyone else had six. That's why at 12:00 they would have only had computer class left and Ed would have had three other classes. In all actuality, Ed was going to cut those classes anyway because he didn't want to miss out on this golden opportunity. He already had three grand in cash that he didn't tell anybody about and he also had work that he was going to have a couple of young boys to knock off for him.

He felt like this would be his side hustle and wasn't going to let anything stop him from making money. He wasn't going to use his Jersey connect until he was almost done with the free work he had taken from Peedi after he murked him and his goons a couple of days ago.

The streets were talking, but they didn't know who did it. At this point, Ed felt as though he had gotten away with it so he was going to live it up. His only regret was that he should have made Peedi take him to his stash house. That way he would have really came up. It was all good though. He would make what he had work.

EJ was walking from the lunch room to meet up with everybody when he saw Yahnise and her gold digging friends standing at their lockers talking. Yahnise was rocking the shit out of her white tennis skirt and pink *Polo* shirt. She had on a pair of pink and white *Air Maxes* and her hair was bone straight hanging down her back.

She looked so good that EJ stood at his locker and stared at her for a while. Her friends were dressed to impress as well. Sonja had on a pair of tights that really made her ass stick out and her other friend Meena was rocking some tight ass *Apple Bottom* jeans with a tight shirt that made her big ass titties stick out. You could honestly say that they were the dream team when it came to the baddest girls in school. EJ only cared about Yahnise though. He wanted her in the worst way and he was determined that one day she would be his.

EJ snapped out of his daydream when Ed hit him on his shoulder. "Yo, you ready to bounce? We have to meet Chan and Wan outside in about ten minutes," Ed said, watching his friend gaze at Yahnise and her girls.

EJ turned and looked at Ed, "Yeah I'm ready. Let's do this." They both walked down the hall.

"Don't worry, once we get our money up those hoes will be dick eating us for real," Ed said to EJ.

"Yo, don't call her a hoe man," EJ said getting mad at Ed for calling Yahnise out of her name. "She just about her money and it ain't anything wrong with that. We don't even know if she is giving any of those niggas some pussy. She is probably just getting what she wants from them," he said, taking one last glance at her.

Ed remained silent while listening to his friend talk out of the side of his neck. He knew how EJ felt about that girl and he hoped that one day his friend would get her.

* * * *

They pulled up at Maria's crib at 12:25 p.m. ready to get the job done. EJ didn't have any dress clothes so he sported the same *Armani* suit again. He wanted to appear as if he was getting money and had a real job.

Maria had called him yesterday and decided that she would let him use her Lexus to go to the bank. She figured that if they saw him pull up in an expensive car that they wouldn't think twice about him cashing a $2,700.00 check.

Once everybody was at the round table, Maria went over the plan again. She wanted to make sure everybody was on point and ready for action.

"Okay gentleman, let's go get this money. EJ and Ed, y'all will go to the PNC Bank on Garrett Road. Chan and Wan you two will go to the TD Bank on State Road," Maria said making sure that they all understood. "I will be here with the information just in case they call."

Everyone got up and left the house to handle their business. Maria said a silent prayer hoping that everything went according to plan. This would set off what would be the beginning of their get-rich scheme.

* * * *

EJ and Ed arrived at PNC Bank on Garrett Road at 1:30 p.m. From looking at the cars in the parking lot, the bank didn't seem that crowded.

"Okay dawg, this is the moment of truth. I will hopefully be in and out of here fast. If anything looks crazy out here, text me ASAP; okay?" EJ said, looking at Ed with his face as serious as ever.

"I got you on speed dial so don't worry about nothing. Just go handle your business so we can start making some real money," Ed said, giving EJ a pound.

EJ stepped out of the car and fixed his suit jacket as he walked up to the doors of the bank. He would be lying if he said he wasn't nervous. When he walked in, it was only one person ahead of him. He walked over and stood in line waiting to be called.

The "NEXT" light sign flashed on and EJ walked up to the teller.

"Good afternoon sir. How can I help you?" the teller asked in a friendly manner. She was a white girl around the age of twenty-five or twenty-eight years old. She looked very nice so EJ's nervousness subsided slightly.

"Yes, I'm here to cash my paycheck," EJ said in a professional manner while looking at the teller.

Then he took the checkout of the envelope and grabbed a pen to endorse it. After EJ signed the check, he passed it to the teller, stood there, and watched her closely. She looked at the check, then up at him with a smile and said, "Can I have your ID please, Mr. Johnson?"

"Oh yeah, sorry about that," EJ said pulling out his ID and handing it to the teller. "It's been a long day at the office and I still have a lot to do," EJ said smiling at her. She smiled back and started punching in some numbers into her computer. EJ waited patiently wondering what she was doing.

The teller looked up from her computer screen and said, "Mr. Johnson please give me a few minutes to verify this check. I will be right back and I won't be long." Then she got up and walked to the back to the manager's officer.

EJ felt like he was about to have a nervous breakdown. He was thinking about running out of there. After about five minutes, the teller came back out with a smile on her face. EJ relaxed a little when she handed him back his ID and said, "Sorry it took me so long Mr. Johnson. When we receive a check over $1,500.00, we have to verify it."

EJ took a mental note of that so he would remember that whenever they cashed a check, they shouldn't exceed that amount.

"How would you like your money sir? Do you want big or small bills?" she asked opening her cash drawer.

"All large bills please," EJ said with a smile. *"Everything seems to be working out fine, but I can't wait to get out of here,"* he said to himself." The teller placed the money in an envelope and passed it to him. "Have a nice day and please come again," she said as she waited for the next customer.

EJ left there with a big smile on his face. He jumped in the car and started it up before looking at Ed. "We did it baby boy. Send the text to Chan and Wan to let them know that it's a go," he said, holding up the envelope full of money.

Ed gave EJ a pound and made the text to Chan. "That's all it is my nigga! Let's get to the next bank and try another one," Ed said, as they pulled out of the bank parking lot, and headed for the next bank.

Chan and Wan also successfully completed their transaction. EJ and Ed were heading to the bank that Chan and Wan was leaving. Chan and Wan were on their way to the bank that EJ and Ed had just left. They switched so that they could stay in the same area and get back to Maria's crib around the same time.

* * * *

Around 4:00, everyone had made it back to Maria's house without any problems. They had cashed all four checks and now they were sitting at the table counting their money. The total came up to $6,000.00 and they split it five ways which means they had $1,200.00 apiece.

That was a nice amount of money for EJ because he never had that much money at one time before. When he saw Ed with that kind of money, he was giving it to Peedi.

If EJ would have sold drugs with Ed, he would have a lot of money by now, but he didn't want to go that route. He thought he could do better and if this worked out as he was hoping it would then he would be doing better. The only problem now was trying to convince his friend to leave the drug game alone altogether. EJ wasn't a dummy. He knew that Ed was still selling drugs. He thought if he put him on to this, then he would quit. The bad part about that was that Ed did not intend to do any of that.

"Good job everybody. I'm glad to see that everything went according to plan and no one got into any trouble. This is just the beginning of what is yet to come," Maria said while they all sat around the table. "We are going to wait a couple of days and then we will hit up the banks again. This time we will do more so that our cut will increase. Once we all get to a nice figure, then we can expand a little."

"I think we should bring the four people in on this now. That way we could hit even more banks," EJ said as he looked around the table. "We don't have to split it in half with the people that we hire. They can get a percentage of whatever they cash. I have four people in mind if everybody agrees. We can add them in as soon as next week," EJ said waiting for a response.

"Don't you think it's too early to add people now? What if they can't handle the pressure and they get snatched up," Wan said, looking at EJ.

"Well we won't have to worry about the people that I have in mind folding under pressure. They do schemes on a regular basis, just not at this magnitude, but to respect your wishes I'll hold off for a few weeks before I bring them in. That way we can first make sure that the plan is fool proof. Is that cool with everybody?" EJ said as each person shook their head in agreement.

"Well now that, that's settled, let's go and enjoy some of this money. Don't spend it too fast," Maria said and then laughed because she knew that as fast as they spent it, they could make it right back.

CHAPTER 9

For the next couple of weeks, the team hit up over twelve different banks, cashing thirty checks. They never went over $1,500.00 because EJ remembered what the teller had said to him about verifying the money. In total, they had made $45,000.00 in two weeks. That was $9,000.00 apiece. EJ had stepped up his game by buying brand new clothes and throwing all of his old stuff away. He only purchased top of the line clothes, all courtesy of Denver. She boosted clothes, shoes, and sneakers for him and he paid her good. He even told her that he would have a job for her soon. She thought he was selling drugs because of all the money he had been spending with her, but he assured her that wasn't the case.

Someone else was starting to take notice of EJ's change in appearance too. Yahnise noticed that he had been dressing better in the last week. She wanted to know what he was doing, but she didn't say anything. When he came to class the last couple of days, he was wearing brand new everything. Her curiosity was getting the best of her. "I wonder what that dude is doing because he looks like new money now," she said to her friends.

"He is probably selling drugs or something," Meana said, as they watched EJ leave with Chan after computer class.

"What are you going to do for Christmas vacation?" EJ asked Chan as they walked outside.

"We have to come up with something that will get us some more money. We have hit all of these banks and we are still not making a lot of money," Chan said as they stood and talked by Chan's car.

"I do have something we could do to get paid a whole lot more money. It will require us to extend the amount of the checks. We can get a couple of people to deposit checks into their accounts, wait three days, and then withdraw the money out of their account. We can start doing this after the New Year's if you are willing to take that change," EJ said, waiting for Chan's response.

Chan thought about it and said, "We will talk about it in our next meeting with Maria. It sounds good, but you know there will be some risk with it." Chan was now looking at EJ with numbers flowing through his head.

"Don't worry because if we get the right people with accounts, it will go smoothly. We will just have to wait and find out," EJ said as he shook hands with Chan and headed over to his aunt's car. He hollered to Chan, "I will see you tomorrow so that we can hit these joints up."

"Later E," Chan said, as he jumped in his car and pulled off. EJ followed him out of the parking lot and went to the bank on 23rd and Snyder called Beneficial. He wanted to start a bank account to hold his money.

* * * *

Meanwhile over in North Philly on 23rd and Diamond Street, Ed was sitting in his car talking to a young boy named Twan. "So how is business," he asked while puffing on a Dutch.

"I'm almost out of the pack you gave me so you can hit me with another one," Twan said waiting for Ed to pass him the Dutch.

Twan had been knocking off the stolen drugs that Ed had taken from Peedi. He had been working for Ed for a week now and he was really showing his loyalty. Ed wanted to lock North Philly down, but first he had to get more workers, so his only concern right now was Diamond Street.

"Well today is your lucky day young boy," Ed said as he grabbed the shopping bag from the back seat and passed it to Twan. "This is a ¼ of a key. How fast can you make this disappear?"

Twan's eyes lit up as he looked at the coke. "Man I'm on it right now. Holler at me in a couple of days and I'll have all of your money," he said getting out of the car so he could take care of business.

The quarter key that Ed gave Twan came from his Jersey connect. He had visited him earlier and he hit him off with the work on consignment. All he had to do now was wait for Twan to take care of that and he would hit him up again. Between the money that Ed made with his best friend and the money he was going to make from the coke, he was doing great.

EJ had already put a down payment on a new car. He wanted a 2007 *Buick Lacrosse* that this mechanic named Tony on 58th and Woodland was selling. It was clean and it didn't have that many miles on it. He didn't want to pay him the money in full because he didn't want EJ to know he had all that money.

As he was pulling down Diamond Street, he saw this light skin girl with a fat ass walk into the Chinese store. He pulled up and parked the car. Then he hurriedly jumped out, and went into the store to see what was up with her. She caught him staring at her as she paid for her food and asked, "Do you have a problem staring at my ass?"

Ed looked at her and said, "As a matter of fact I do. I can't let someone who looks that fine pay for her own food." He pulled out a knot of money, peeled off a twenty dollar bill, and gave it to the cashier.

Her eyes lit up at the sight of his knot. "Well thank you baller," she said never taking her eyes off of his money.

"No problem Shorty. Where are you about to go right now?" he asked as the clerk gave him his change.

"I'm about to go in the house and relax, I guess. Why? What's up with you?" she said seductively.

"First off, what is your name and secondly, I would like to go with you if you can have some company. I don't want your man to beat me up for coming to your house," he said playfully.

She smiled and said, "My name is Tamera and I don't have a man. You can come keep me company for a while, but my mom will be home by 8:00 so you can only stay until 7:00."

Tamara started walking out the door and Ed looked down at his phone. It was only 4:30 so he said fuck it and followed her out the door. "Where do you live at?"

"On the next block so you can leave your car parked there if you want. There is never anywhere to park on my block," Tamera said as her and Ed walked to her crib.

* * * *

When they entered the house, Tamara took off her shoes and told Ed to get comfortable while she changed her clothes. Ed watched as she switched upstairs, making her ass jiggle in her sweatpants.

"You can put some music on and I'll be down in ten minutes," she hollered from the top of the stairs.

Ed turned the radio on and Nelly's "Drop Down and Get Your Eagle On" was on the radio so he let it play. He looked around at all the pictures and noticed that all of the girls in the pictures with her were bad too. He thought to himself, *"They must be her sisters."* He continued to look at the other pictures when she came back downstairs wearing a skimpy robe that barely covered her ass.

"Do you want to smoke this Dutch with me?" Ed asked as he pulled it out of his jacket. He went over and sat on the couch and Tamara came and sat beside him.

"Yeah, spark that shit up," she said as she leaned back on the couch. From where Ed was sitting, he could see her lace panties and they looked like they were being swallowed up by her ass. He knew she must have been wearing a thong.

He had met this girl just about fifteen minutes ago and already he was about to get some pussy.

After they smoked the Dutch, she asked him if he wanted her to dance for him. Ed shook his head and Tamara put on stripper music and began coming out of her robe.

Ed didn't know it, but Tamara was a stripper at Bottom Up right off of Roosevelt Boulevard. When she saw all that money, she was thrilled to take Ed back to her crib. She thought if she performed for him, he would break her off.

She had on a red lace thong with a matching bra. Her titties were not too small, but they weren't big either. They were just right. She began dancing seductively and then got on top of Ed and began grinding on him. He grabbed her ass and squeezed it while she rode him.

After about five minutes of lap dancing, Ed wanted some pussy. He pulled her thong to the side and put his finger in her pussy. She was very wet and he began to stroke his finger in and out of her.

After a few seconds, she stopped him and said, "If you want some of this, you are going to have to pay for it." She stood up to see what his response would be.

Ed looked at her and then pulled out his knot. He peeled off one hundred dollars and sat it on the table in front of him. She smiled at him and said, "You are gonna want to spend more than that after I'm done with you!"

She got down on her knees and unzipped Ed's pants. She then pulled out his dick and in one swift motion; she took him in her mouth. When she pulled him out of her mouth, to his surprise a condom was on his dick.

"Damn ma! How the fuck did you do that?" Ed said, looking amazed and turned on at the same time.

"I told you I'm gonna turn your ass out. You haven't seen nothing yet," Tamara said as she began sucking the Ed's dick. She was a deep throat specialist, and took all of him in her mouth without gagging. Ed was turned out already and he hadn't even fucked her yet.

Then he told Tamara to lie on the couch. She put her face in the pillow and tooted her ass up in the air. He pulled his pants and boxers down to his ankles and pulled her thong to the side. He entered her from the back and his dick slid right in with no problem.

"Oh shit Daddy! Tear this pussy up!" Tamara begged and moaned as she bit down on her bottom lip as Ed's dick slid in and out of her wet pussy.

Ed started with medium speed strokes as he listened to Tamara moan, watched her fat ass jiggle and bounce back and forth with each stroke.

"Throw that shit back ma!" Ed demanded as his strokes started to speed up. Like a good little girl, Tamara did as she was told, and threw her ass back, enjoying every stroke.

Ed spread both of Tamara's ass cheeks apart as he continued to thrust his dick into her hot sopping wet pussy until he couldn't take it anymore and filled his condom with semen.

"Damn girl! I think I'm in love!" Ed said as he sat on the couch and began taking the condom off. Before he could finish, Tamara was already pulling it off with her mouth. She took the whole condom off with her mouth and spit on the floor. Before Ed could say a word, she was already trying to bring his dick back to life.

"Damn! You are one nasty freaky bitch and I think I'm going to have to keep you around," he said while watching her go to work on his penis.

"I told you I would have you sprung," Tamara said looking up from sucking his dick.

They ended up fucking again until he had to leave. She didn't want him to go, but her mom was on her way home. Truth be told, he had also turned her ass out. When they finished, they exchanged numbers and Ed left for home.

* * * *

Ed arrived at his crib an hour later and went straight to his room. When he unlocked his door, he noticed that he had forgotten to put his money up. *"Oh shit! I'm glad I have that lock on my door,"* he said to himself as he went over to count all of the money on his bed. He now had twelve thousand dollars in cash and that wasn't even including the money from Twan that he still had in the car. He thought to himself that he better buy a safe so he could keep his money protected. That was the first thing he was going to do after they did their thing tomorrow.

For now though, he needed some much deserved rest. Nobody was home but him so he took a shower and went to bed early.

CHAPTER 10

July 4, 2009

It had been seven months since Maria had formed her alliance. All of them had graduated high school last month except for Ed who had dropped out of school after he locked down a few blocks in North Philly. He had his own team of killers and drug dealers. They were all young boys with ages ranging from fifteen to seventeen. They all wanted to be like him so they followed his every word.

EJ and the rest of the team had made a tremendous come up as well. They now had a team of casher's and depositors. All in all, they had a team that was fifteen strong, including the five that started this operation.

They were making money out of their asses. It was the fourth of July and everybody was having a cookout. EJ and Ed decided they were going to go to the cookout in Fairmount Park. That's where all of the women were so they wanted to be there. They both had purchased motorcycles for the summer. EJ had a 600 CBR that was kitted up to make it fast as a 750. He was a little scared of bikes, but since he had just learned how to ride, he wanted one.

Ed had a Yamaha 1100, which was extremely fast. They both wore wife beaters with *True Religion* jean shorts. Ed had his tattoos on display for everyone to see. EJ didn't have any tattoos, but his muscles made up for all that. He was cut up like a bag of dope from working out the past five months.

When they pulled up to the park, all the girls were eye balling them. EJ noticed one in particular. It was Yahnise! Her and her girls were looking good as hell. She had on a black *Monki* mini-skirt, a white *Patta Distribution* shirt, and a pair of white Nike *Air Force One*'s. Sonja was sporting a *Steffe Dress* with a pair of *Eric Rutberg* wedge sandals and Meana had on a *Karen Miller* dress with a pair of *DeeFind* platform heels.

They were definitely getting all of the attention. EJ didn't think that he would see anybody else there as bad as them. He knew every nigga there had probably tried to come at them by now.

Yahnise watched EJ as he was talking to everybody and he kept staring at her as well. As he and Ed walked pass them, one of her girls hollered out, "Look at y'all get money niggas. I see y'all finally stepped your game up, huh!"

Before EJ could say anything, Ed spoke up. "Oh so now you want to talk to us; huh? Before you didn't have shit to say so don't bother to say shit now!"

The girls couldn't believe that Ed had just talked to them like that. They all turned and started walking the other way. Yahnise turned around and looked at EJ as if she wanted to say something, but she didn't. He watched as they mingled with everyone else.

* * * *

Later that night, it was time to watch the fireworks. Ed had left because he met some shorty and he wanted to take her home and fuck her. EJ stayed and chilled with a couple of people. As he stood there watching the fireworks, he noticed Yahnise standing over by herself. He thought this was his chance to say something to her or else he may never get the chance again.

He walked up and stood beside her while still watching the show. "Yahnise I would like to apologize for my friend's rude outburst earlier," EJ said as he looked at her. "I know it might not mean much, but I've liked you since we were in high school. I knew you would never give someone like me a chance unless I was getting money. Well I'm living a good life now and I would love to take you out sometime if you are interested," EJ said waiting for an answer.

Yahnise turned and looked at him. She couldn't deny that he had come up by the way he carried himself now.

"What makes you think that I like people with money or will only talk to people that can buy me things? I knew you liked me, but I never said anything because you always acted as if you were scared to approach me. You see me with all of this expensive stuff on and assume that I got it from a baller. Well just so you know; my mom and dad bought all of this stuff for me. In fact, the niggas that I did talk to never gave me anything. I didn't want them to think they would get something back in return," she said while looking back at the fireworks.

EJ was shocked because he assumed that she was a gold digger. "I guess I misjudged you and your friends; huh?"

"No, my friends only fuck with ballers, but I'm not like that," she said giving him a smile. "I would like to apologize to you as well for my friends treating you like that when you held the door open that day in school. I should have said something a while ago, but every time you seen me after that, you went the other way."

"Well I would really like to get to know you, Yahnise. I was shy before, but now I have a little bit of confidence," EJ said smiling.

They stood, talking while watching the rest of the show. As they talked, they realized that they had a lot in common. It was dark outside and the fireworks were over. Yahnise gave EJ her phone number and he did the same. He walked her to her car and opened the door for her to get in before shutting it.

"Well, I had a nice time talking to you. Make sure you call me when you get home so I will know that you made it there safely and be careful on that bike," Yahnise said, starting her car.

"I'll do that and you also be careful and don't give any strangers a ride," EJ said, and they both broke into laughter.

He watched her as she pulled off and then jumped up and down from excitement as he went to jump on his bike and head home, thinking about her the entire way.

* * * *

Ed woke up at around 1:00 in the morning. The little shorty that he had bagged earlier at the park was lying next to him butt naked with the sheet only covering half of her body. He was about to wake her up for another round of fucking when his cell phone rang.

Ed grabbed his phone off of the dresser and seen that it was Twan calling him. "Hey! What's good nigga?" he said sitting up on the edge of the bed.

"Yo! We just got robbed! They hit the stash house about five minutes ago and they killed three of our workers," Twan said sounding hysterical.

"Whoa! Whoa! Slow down nigga. Who hit the stash house and what happened to the workers?" Ed said walking out of his bedroom and going into his sister's bedroom so no one could hear his conversation.

Twan calmed down and said, "Some niggas came through in a white van and took everything in the stash house. They killed BoBo, Shank, and Peewee. They also left a note talking about this is only the beginning if you don't shut this operation down." Twan paused for a minute to catch his breath because he was talking a mile a minute. "I was just pulling up when they were pulling off. I ran in the spot and Peewee was still alive. He is the one who told me what happened before he went into shock and flat-lined right in my arms! This is fucked up!" he said, sounding as if he was almost in tears and mad as hell.

"Yo, round up everybody and meet me at the spot. Make sure

everybody is locked and loaded. It's war time!" Ed said, as he ended the call.

He ran back in his room and started putting on his black jeans and a black hoodie. Then he grabbed his black Timbs out of the closet. "Wake up Shorty. I have to go. It's an emergency," Ed said shaking the girl on her ass.

She woke up and dressed quickly when she saw the look on Ed's face.

"I will call you tomorrow night and we can hook up and go out to dinner or something," he said as he put on his bullet proof vest.

After Ed showed her out, he went to his basement where he kept his guns. He grabbed the AK47 assault rifle and two 9mm's with the extended clip. Then he quickly left his house and jumped in his car heading to the spot.

* * * *

When Ed got there, all the goons were already there waiting on him. He had about fifteen killers on his team and they were locked and loaded. "Did anybody say who these niggas was that hit the spot," he asked, pacing the floor.

"Yeah it was that nigga YG's people," one of his lieutenants said. YG was not only doing the chop shop thing, but he had some blocks on lock since Peedi had died. Now he was trying to take Ed's blocks also and he wasn't having that.

"Okay! Then it's time to pay this motherfucker a visit! Everybody in that place dies tonight. If anybody is left standing, the person that missed will have to deal with me; understand? Ed said looking around the room at everyone.

There was silence.

"Okay, let's roll out," he said, heading for the door.

Everybody jumped in four different cars. Ed couldn't believe that, that nigga YG would try to take over his spot. Then on top of that, he had the audacity to kill three of his best men. A sin that bad could not go unpunished. If it was war that he wanted, then it was war that he was going to get. The bad part about it was that he knew where his chop shop was located and he also knew where the nigga rested his head.

Ed dialed Gene's number to make sure he wasn't with him. "Yo, what's up nigga? Where you at?" Ed asked.

"I'm chilling with my Shorty right now. Why? What's up?" Gene said sitting on the couch.

"That nigga YG hit my spot tonight and killed three of my men. Now I'm on my way to see that bitch ass nigga," Ed said mad as shit.

"Yo, where you at now? I'm going to meet you so I can ride out with you," Gene said strapping up.

"We're on our way to his shop right now," Ed said, hitting the blunt from his man.

"Okay, I'm out the door right now. I'll be there in about fifteen minutes. If all hell breaks loose before then, make sure your men don't fire at me because I will be coming with my shit blazing," Gene said running to and jumping inside his car.

"Okay, peace nigga! See you when I see you," Ed said hanging up.

* * * *

YG was at his shop laughing about the come-up he had just made. He was a greedy and stingy motherfucker. The only people he treated right were the ones in his own circle. If you weren't in his immediate circle then you could get it. That's why not only did he hit Ed's spot, but he had hit some other nigga in Chester too.

"How much did we get from those bitch ass niggas?" YG asked one of his soldiers.

"All together with both licks, we scored about $60,000.00 in cash and three and a quarter of work," the goon told him.

"Alright, that's good. Now maybe those niggas will leave the area and never come back."

He never did like Ed. Ever since that night that he came to his shop with Gene, he knew he was a cocky son-of-a-bitch. That's why he never did business with Gene after that. Gene tried to bring some more work his way, but he turned it down. That infuriated Gene, but he wouldn't try shit due to the fact that YG had about twenty soldiers around him at all times.

"Okay, let's party! Bring the bitches in here so we can get some lap dances," YG said, trying to enjoy himself. He wasn't spending his money so he didn't care that they were about to blow a few thousand on some pussy.

* * * *

Ed and his soldiers arrived at the shop and to their surprise; they heard loud music as if they were having a party.

"Okay, when we go in here, we are to go in fast and don't leave nothing behind or no one standing," Ed said cocking his AK.

Before they could pull off towards the garage, Gene pulled up. "We are gonna have to ram through the gate and once we do that, all hell is going to break loose," he said as he grabbed the AR15 out of his trunk.

"Alright fellas, let's go let these bitch boys know who they are fucking with!" Ed said as they jumped back in their cars and pulled off.

* * * *

YG was on the couch drinking Cîroc while a white stripper gave him good head. Everybody was enjoying themselves until they heard a loud bang and gunfire coming from several different types of guns at the same time.

BLOC! BLOC! BLOC! BLOC!
POP! POP! POP! POP!
BOC! BOC! BOC! BOC!

Everybody jumped, ran for cover, and grabbed their weapons.

YG tossed the girl off of him and grabbed his Tech-9 from under the pillow.

"Who the fuck is that?! Everybody strap the fuck up and get those bitch ass niggas!"

YG ran over and hit his video monitor and all he saw was his men outside shooting it out with what looked like twenty niggas in all black. All of the men had on masks so their faces couldn't be seen, but YG knew who it was. He didn't think that they would retaliate this fast. *"How in the hell did they even know it was me?"* he thought to himself as he ran for the area where his soldiers were at war.

He was going to ride with his boys no matter what!

BOOM! That was the sound of the door being kicked in. Two niggas ran in with guns blazing, but YG already had the drop on them. He hit them both in the head killing them before they even hit the ground.

He then realized that he was losing the battle so he made his way out the back door and jumped into one of his cars and made his escape.

* * * *

Bodies covered the place. Ed and Gene were now in the office looking for YG, but he was gone.

"Let's get the fuck out of here!" Ed yelled as he heard sirens from a distance. They all ran out and jumped in their cars and got out of that area before the cops came.

After all of that shooting, they had killed everybody except YG. They had rocked eight of his men during that commotion.

Ed vowed that he would get that nigga if it were the last thing he did. He just didn't know when.

CHAPTER 11

Two weeks had passed since EJ and Yahnise finally started talking. They talked on the phone until four in the morning almost every night and sometimes even falling asleep in each other's ears. They were becoming close, and had made plans to go out on the weekend.

For now, it was time for EJ to get back to business. They were all at Maria's house, planning their next project. Everybody was in attendance except for Ed. He had called earlier and said he was on his way. That was about twenty minutes ago. Just when they were about to begin the meeting, he walked in.

"Sorry I'm late. I had a busy night and I over slept," he said, taking a seat.

EJ looked at him, but didn't say anything. It wasn't the time or place for him to question his friend.

"Okay, well let's get down to business," Maria said. This was her usual meeting starter. "What we are going to do today is hit at least ten banks with checks that we will cash. Then at the same time, we will also deposit ten checks at these same banks. Therefore, I need Ed to take your two workers out to Jersey. Chan you need to take your three workers out to Chester. Wan you will go out to Delaware, and EJ you will hit this area with your three workers," she said as she went over to her desk and picked up some envelopes with the checks that EJ and Chan had printed earlier.

"Each envelope contains two checks," EJ said, standing up. "There is one in the amount of $1,500.00 for the person cashing it and one in the amount of $9,000.00 for the person that is depositing it," he said, looking as everyone's mouths opened.

"You sure about 9G's?" Ed questioned looking shocked. "That's a lot of money!"

"Where have you been boy? That's what we are about now, making money! If you had paying attention, you would have noticed that every check has went up except the ones that get cashed immediately. The names are on each check along with the bank symbol, so make sure the right person gets the right check," EJ said, as he opened his envelope to make sure that his three people's names were spelled right.

He had recruited Denver, Shannon, and one of their friends named Tiffany. Tiffany and Shannon had bank accounts, so their job was easy. Denver on the other hand had to go in the bank. Since she had to do that, EJ would take her to three different banks so that she would be able to do $4,500.00 instead of $1,500.00. Out of that, she would keep the last check to herself. He also kind of liked Denver, but business was business. Tiffany and Shannon would make $1,500.00 off each one that they deposited.

"Okay, let's get out of here and handle our business," EJ said getting ready to leave. "Maria, I'm going to need one of your cars, please. I'm getting my own car next week," he said looking at Maria.

"Sure, just take the Lexus and I'll see you when you get back," she said, as she watched everyone leave.

* * * *

Everyone had to pick up their people from their usual meeting spot at. When EJ pulled up to Denver's crib on 71st Street, they were all standing outside waiting on him. "Okay girls, let's go make this money," he said, as they all got in ready for business.

"Once we get to the first bank, we'll do the same thing that we have been doing. Denver you will go in the bank and cash your check while I take Shannon through the drive thru."

"So when will we be getting paid for this job?" Tiffany asked, looking at her check.

"I will bring everybody their money tomorrow so that y'all can do y'all daily shopping," EJ said, smiling at Tiffany. He knew they never paid for anything. That money was for if they ever got caught, they could say that they were going to buy the merchandise and prove that they had money for it.

"Okay, let's get this over with then," Shannon said from the backseat. She was always the quiet one while Denver was always the loud and crazy one.

"Oh, I forgot to tell all of y'all that y'all are now on salary. Everybody will be making $1,800.00 every two weeks. We will do these three times a week on Monday, Wednesday, and Friday. Everybody will get paid on Saturday," EJ told them, as they pulled up to the bank.

"That's what's up E! I need that money," Denver said, as they all started cheering. Little did they know that they really weren't making that much money off their jobs. By them doing it this way, they didn't have to pay them off every check now. That was more money in EJ's and the others pockets. Off of three days of work, EJ and his partners will make $27,000.00

* * * *

Everything went well; EJ dropped everybody off and headed back to Maria's crib. When he got there, he rang the doorbell, but no one answered. He knew that Maria was home because all of her cars were parked in the driveway. The butler wasn't there because she had sent him to pick up something in New York. He wasn't scheduled to arrive back until later on tonight.

He walked around to the side doors and went inside. "Maria, where are you?" he yelled as he headed through the door.

While he was walking, he dialed her cell phone and she answered after the fourth ring, "hello."

"I'm in your crib right now. Where are you at?" EJ said, now standing in the den. "I'm in the hot tub relaxing. You're back quicker than everyone else is. Did everything go alright?" she asked sounding a little concerned.

"Yeah, we handled our business and I took them back home and then came straight here. I didn't want to keep your car too long," he said, heading in the direction of her hot tub. "Can I come in or are you naked?"

"Nigga get your ass in here. I'm out now," she said hanging up her cell phone. When EJ walked in there, Maria had on a lime green thong with a matching bra. He was standing in the door stuck in place watching Maria put on her robe. When she turned around, she looked at EJ and said, "What's wrong with you? What? You never seen a woman in her panties before?"

"Stop playing girl. It's just that I have never seen you like this," EJ said, taking a seat next to the hot tub.

"Well get used to it because I'm not afraid to show off this beautiful figure," she said, spinning around like a model.

EJ laughed and told her about all of the events of today. He even told her about the payroll that he and Chan had created. She thought it was a smart decision.

"Well I'm about to make me something to eat since nobody is here to cook for me. Would you like something to eat?" she asked, as she starting walking towards the kitchen.

The whole time EJ stared at her ass while she walked in that little ass robe that barely covered anything. "*You just don't know*," he mumbled to himself.

"Did you say something?" Maria asked, as she stopped and turned around.

"I said sure, I would love to taste your food," he said smiling. "It will be nice to have a beautiful woman cook for me for a change."

A smirk danced on Maria's lips. "Are you just telling me what I want to hear or are you serious?"

"I don't play games and you know that by now," EJ said as he sat at the kitchen table.

"Hold up. Let me see if you are lying to me or not," Maria said as she looked at him. Before she got a chance to say something slick, EJ stood up, pulled her towards him, and kissed her passionately.

He paused for a moment and said, "I always wanted to do that, but we're partners and we can't mix business with pleasure."

"Well for the next few minutes while we are the only two here, we are just two people having a little fun," Maria said, while kissing him again.

A few seconds later, Maria's hands were down EJ's shorts fondling his dick. She quickly made him hard as a brick.

"Let me see what you are working with," EJ slurred.

Maria complied quickly, as she led EJ to the living room and pushed him down on the couch. She hurriedly let her robe fall to the floor and she slowly and sensually began gyrating her hips. She unbuttoned her bra and let it fall to the floor. Then she palmed her full breast and pulled on her nipples as she continued to entertain EJ.

"You gonna just sit there and watch me or are you gonna handle your business? We don't have that much time before the other's return," Maria said, in a challenging tone.

EJ immediately pulled out his dick. "Don't talk me to death. I can handle anything that comes my way."

EJ sat back and watched Maria take his dick into her warm mouth and wrap her juicy lips around it. As EJ began to fuck Maria's mouth, she felt her pussy began to warm and moisten.

Maria's mouth felt so good that EJ grabbed the back of her head and begged her not to stop, as sliding it in and out of her mouth.

"You like that Daddy?" Maria asked as she pushed her thong to the side, rubbed her clit, and then stuck her fingers in EJ's mouth. After a few more minutes of sucking, EJ couldn't take it anymore. He aggressively turned Maria around, pulled her thong off, and reached in his pocket and pulled out a condom. He quickly rolled the condom on and entered her pulsating pussy.

"Oh shit!" she sighed and panted in pleasure as she took the dick as best she could.

"Don't cry now smart ass," EJ grumbled as he slid deeper and deeper inside her tight hole.

"That's right! I want you to fuck me just like that Papi!" Maria said through clenched teeth, as she threw her pussy back at EJ. He grabbed Maria's waist as he watched her ass slap back and forth against his torso. After about twenty minutes of getting her back dug out, Maria crawled away from EJ's back shots.

"What's wrong?" EJ asked, looking like he was about to nut.

"I want to ride that dick Papi," she said in a sexually charged tone, as she pushed EJ back on the couch and sat on top of him guiding his dick into her pussy walls.

After about ten minutes of riding his dick, Maria came for the third time. EJ couldn't take it any longer and he busted right after that. They both sat there for a couple of minutes before Maria got up and went to put some clothes on before the rest of their crew returned.

EJ did the same, but the whole time he was fucking Maria, he was pretending it was Yahnise. He really had it bad for Yahnise. He was going to take her out on Saturday and hopefully seal the deal.

CHAPTER 12

December 24, 2010

EJ and Yahnise have been together for over a year. EJ had moved out of his aunt's house and into a three bedroom house in Upper Darby, on a little block right off of West Chester Pike called Berbro Road. The house was decorated beautifully thanks to Yahnise who had also picked it out herself. After everything was done, she had moved in with EJ. They had become inseparable and spent all of their time together except when EJ was doing business.

He had a two car garage where he kept his Range Rover and the Nissan Armada truck that he had purchased for Yahnise for her birthday last January. He loved her more than anything in the whole world did and there was nothing that he wouldn't do for her.

He had even gone as far as putting her name on his bank account so that they now had a joint account. He made sure that he told her of all deposits so she could keep their books updated.

It was Christmas Eve and they were getting ready for a Christmas party over at Yahnise sister's house. Her sister Nyia had moved out Pottstown with her husband Chris who owned a car dealership out there.

EJ had something planned for Yahnise that night and he had decided that it would be even better if he did it at the party.

"Are you ready baby? You know how bad traffic is on I-76 this time of night," EJ said, waiting for Yahnise to get ready.

"Here I come now. I'm putting on my shoes now and I have to grab my sister and niece's presents," Yahnise said, yelling down the stairs.

"Okay, I'll be in the car. I have to put all of the stuff for your nephews in there," EJ said, heading for the door.

They had decided that EJ would get the boys stuff and Yahnise would get the girls stuff. By the time they were on their way, the Range Rover was filled to the tee with presents. They over did it when it came to those kids and there was nothing that was too much for them.

* * * *

When they pulled up to Nyia's house, the party was already jumping. They had so many family and friends there that it was hard to find a parking spot. When they walked in, everyone was enjoying themselves and having a good time. Yahnise went to find her sister while EJ was getting a soda and chilling with Chris.

"I'm going to pop the question tonight after twelve," EJ told Chris, as they listened to Meek Millz play on the stereo.

"That's what I'm talking about nigga!" Chris said with a huge smile on his face. "I got that other thing down the street ready whenever you are so just let me know and I'll bring it up here."

"Thanks man and you will have that check tomorrow morning," EJ said, as he went to mingle before the big surprise.

* * * *

It was 11:55 p.m. and everyone was enjoying themselves, dancing and drinking. EJ made sure that Yahnise didn't drink any liquor that night because he didn't want anything clouding her judgment.

Ed was there with his new fiancé, Tamara. They had become a lot closer since that one night encounter. She had even moved in his new house out in Paulsboro, New Jersey. They had a nice four bedroom house on Washington Street. Tamara had him so sprung that he popped the big question after only three months.

Chris slowly pulled up in the driveway with the surprise for Yahnise. Everyone was in the house opening up gifts now. EJ was waiting for the right moment to handle his business. They had even decided to let the kids stay up late to open up some of their presents.

It was now 12:30 a.m. and everyone was starting to calm down, so EJ thought this was the right time to step up and do what he had wanted to do for so long now. Everyone was in the same room when Chris came in and turned the music off so that EJ could speak.

"Can I have everybody's attention, please?" EJ asked as he stood in the middle of the floor. Everyone stopped talking and gave him their undivided attention.

"I just want to thank Nyia and Chris for inviting me to this party. At first I was going to go out to the Poconos, but I'm glad that I didn't because I wouldn't be able to share the good news with everybody," EJ said, trying to think of the right words to say.

"Yahnise, come here baby," he said, holding his hand out for her. She walked over to him and grabbed his hand. He looked into her eyes and said, "Ever since the first time I laid eyes on you at school, I knew that you were the one for me. I thought that you would never go for someone like me which is why it took me so long to even try to approach you. Ever since that night we shared watching fireworks at Fairmount Park, my whole like has changed. I never thought anyone could bring me as much joy as I feel when I'm with you. I love you more than life itself!"

EJ got down on one knee and pulled a little black box from his pocket. Everyone was in shock; even Yahnise who started breathing heavy as tears formed in her eyes.

EJ opened the box, took the ring out, and grabbed her hand again. "Yahnise I would like to spend the rest of my life with you. I promise to always keep you happy and protect you. Will you do me the honors of being my wife? In other words Yahnise, will you marry me?"

The whole house was so quiet that you could hear a pend drop. Everyone was waiting on Yahnise to answer. Yahnise's mom, Ms. Pam started crying tears of joy.

Yahnise looked into EJ's eyes as if she was trying to look through his soul. She started crying and said, "Yes! Yes! Yes baby, I will marry you!"

Everyone began clapping and cheering as EJ placed the ten carat, blue diamond ring on her finger. He stood up and kissed his fiancé passionately as everyone continued to cheer.

After the room calmed down a bit, he told her that he had another surprise for her. Before he could say anything she said, "I have a surprise for you too baby."

He looked at her and she said, "We are having a baby." EJ was so shocked that he picked her up and spun her around as they kissed once more.

Yahnise went to the doctor's office two days prior and found out that she was six-weeks pregnant. She wanted to tell him sooner, but decided to wait for the right time. After he proposed to her, she figured the time was right to inform her new husband to be of their soon-to-be-baby. This Christmas was probably one of the best for the both of them.

"Now Mister, what was that other surprise you had for me?" Yahnise asked as she held her arms around his neck.

"Come with me and find out," he said, leading her to the front door. Everyone in the house almost knew what that meant as they ran towards the door behind them to see what he got for her.

"Close your eyes and don't open them until I say so," EJ said, heading her out the door. "Now open them."

When Yahnise opened her eyes, she almost passed out. There in the driveway sat a brand new CLK Mercedes Benz. It was fully black with butterscotch leather interior. The license plate said "YAHNISE" and it had a big ass red bow and ribbon on it.

"Oh my God! Oh my God! This is what I always wanted!" Yahnise yelled, jumping up and down. Just when she thought this night couldn't get any better, he came up with something else.

They stayed for another hour before heading home. EJ left his Range Rover at Nyia's house so that he could ride with his boo in her new car. Chris said that he would drop it off in the morning for him.

That night when they got home, they made love until almost 9:00 that morning. It had to be the best sex that either of them had ever had. EJ had work to do the day after Christmas, but for now he was all hers and no one was going to disturb them.

CHAPTER 13

Two Months Later

Agent Kaplin was sitting in his office working on some tax evasion reports when he received a phone call from the Philadelphia Police Department's Fraud Unit.

"Agent Kaplin, I have a Detective Harris on line one for you. He says he needs to have a word with you," the receptionist said on the PA system.

"I'll take the call now," Agent Kaplin said clicking line one. "This is Special Agent Keith Kaplin. How can I help you?"

"Hi, my name is Detective Harris from the fraud division over here on 8th and Race. I was wondering if you would be interested in sitting in or even handling a case that I have here. It involves fake checks being cashed at a very rapid pace," the Detective said.

"Well, I'll be right there," Agent Kaplin said as he hung up the phone, grabbed his jacket off the back of his chair, and headed for the door.

Agent Kaplin arrived at Central Headquarters ten minutes later. As soon as he walked in and flashed his badge to the desk sergeant, she escorted him to Detective Harris' office.

Detective John Harris was around forty years old. He had been on the force for twenty years and he had been with the fraud division for three of

ERNEST MORRIS

those years. If you didn't ask his age, you would have never known it and you would have thought that he was so old. His body looked good from years of working out. He stood about six feet tall and he had a bald head. He was trying to move up in the ranks so this case right here could make or break him.

When Agent Kaplin walked in, he greeted Detective Harris and sat down in one of the chairs in the front of his desk. "So what can you tell me about these checks being cashed and do you have any suspects?" Agent Kaplin asked.

"Well the only suspects we have are the ones that names were on the checks. We've been trying to locate them, but when we went to the last known address, no one lived there. Now we are back to square one," Detective Harris said.

"So, let's see what you have," Agent Kaplin said looking at the checks on Detective Harris' desk. "Did you run these names through the database?"

"We did and we came up with nothing. They don't even have a traffic ticket which makes me believe that we are dealing with either fake names or some very honest people that got caught up in some kind of scam," the Detective said, looking at the Agent.

"Well that's what we need to find out and fast," the Agent said.

"That's exactly why I called you. We don't have the resources or man power for this type of operation. So, I'm hoping that you will help me out with it," Detective Harris said, sipping his coffee.

"Well I'm going to make some phone calls and put some people on it. I can't promise you anything more than that right now. Let's just see where this leads to because whoever these people are, they have some very good help," Agent Kaplin said as he shook Detective Harris hand and headed for the door. "I'll be in touch," he said and shut the door.

* * * *

Everything was going extremely well for Maria and the crew. They were making so much money doing the checks that they decided to step it up a notch. Now they were making W2's using different companies Tax ID numbers. That alone was making them big bucks. They would design the W2's and then grab people that haven't worked all year and get them to file their taxes using the fake W2's. They only used people who could claim children so they would qualify for Earned Income Tax Credit and the people they chose couldn't have any outstanding debit with the IRS, school loans, or banks.

After they received the fake W2, they would file it through H&R Block or any other quick electronic filing agency. It would take them approximately three days to receive the money. Each transaction was guaranteed no less than $4,000.00. Maria and her crew would take $1,500.00 and the person who filed the W2 would keep the rest of the money.

It was only February and already they had twenty people who had filed so far. Within this one week, they had already acquired thirty thousand dollars. They had people all over the tri-state area doing all types of scams for them. Chan and Wan were in New York right now with workers handling some money transactions. Just on this single trip to New York they had made $200,000.00. They had New York jumping.

EJ was working the New Jersey and Delaware area. He was doing good numbers there because he was selling fake license and ID cards. He really worked harder than anyone else did because he spent all of his time on the computer while everyone else was out in the field. Even when he was home, he was on his laptop preparing work for the next meeting. He was really showing good leadership skills.

Ed was working the Chester area. They had given him that small area because he really didn't seem into his work as everyone else was. Truth be told, Maria only kept him on the team because he was EJ's best friend. His work ethics seemed to be going down lately. Ed was too busy with his drugs to do his job with the crew. That was going to be his downfall little did he know. His numbers were still good for that little area though so it didn't really hurt anything. EJ knew what he doing out in the streets was so he just told his partner to be careful.

They even gave Denver and Shannon a nice position. They had sent them down to Baltimore along with their friend Tiffany to handle some business. The girls were sending $100,000.00 a week back. EJ had set up accounts for everyone and he would deposit their cut into their own account bi-weekly.

Everybody was doing their thing and everybody was eating. As they say, "Whenever you see people eating good, it causes jealousy and envy so more money means more problems."

* * * *

Everyone was going to the club to celebrate EJ's birthday weekend. They went to the Trilogy on 6th and Spring Garden Street. The place was so packed that you couldn't even move around too much. It seemed like people were coming out of the wood works.

EJ, Yahnise, Ed, and Tamara all came together in EJ's new toy. He purchased himself a red Bentley GT with red and black 24" Asanti wheels for his birthday. He felt like he was on the top of the world. He was shitting on niggas.

Maria, Chan, and Wan were all on their way to support their partner. Maria was a little jealous of Yahnise being all up in EJ's arms, but she knew that was his fiancé and future baby mother so she played her position. She and EJ had not had sex since he proposed to Yahnise, but she knew he would want some again.

They were enjoying the music and drinking in the VIP section when a couple of YG niggas came in the club. YG had got the word that they would be there tonight and he wanted revenge on Ed and everyone that was with him. Upon their arrival, they saw Ed and his people enjoying themselves, but they weren't going to spoil it for them. This was not the time so they would just wait for the right time.

"I want to give a shout out to my nigga EJ! Happy 20th birthday and may you have many more," the DJ shouted. Then he put on Rick Ross, "*I'm a Boss*" and the crowd went wild.

"This is your night baby and when we get home, I'm going to fuck you and suck you until you can't cum anymore," Yahnise whispered in EJ's ear, as she sat down on his lap. She felt his dick rise and kissed him on his neck.

Since she has been pregnant, she has been extra horny. It didn't bother EJ because he couldn't get enough of her. He couldn't wait until they got married on July 4th. That was the date that they had finally connected so they decided to use that date to tie the knot.

"Excuse me. I'll be right back. I have to use the bathroom," Ed said, feeling a little tipsy from all the liquor he had been drinking.

As he was walking towards the men's room, YG's goons decided to start some shit. They started walking towards him and before he noticed what was happening, one of them struck him with a bottle. As soon as he hit the floor, all three of the men began stomping him out.

EJ saw all of the commotion and the first thing he thought about was Ed. He immediately jumped up and ran to see what was going on. Chan and Wan followed him. When he got close enough to see his friend on the ground, he burst through the crowd to go help him.

EJ hit the first guy with a three piece, stretching him out easily. Before he could get to another one of the guys, Chan and Wan were on their asses. It quickly turned into a big ass free fall until the bouncers came and broke it up.

They escorted the three men out of the club while EJ, Chan, and Wan helped Ed back to the VIP section. If Ed wasn't so drunk, he probably would have handled all of them, but he was no condition to be fighting.

After all of the commotion, they stayed at the club until closing. They weren't going to let some bullshit stop them from having a good time.

* * * *

"Yo, we just fucked that nigga Ed up in the club until some of his boys came to help him," Bless said. "What do you want us to do now?"

"I want him and whoever he is with dead when they walk out of the club," YG said into the phone.

Since that incident, YG had been laying low trying to formulate a plan to get back at Ed. Therefore, when some chicken head called him and told him that Ed was at Trilogy, he decided to get some sweet revenge.

"Say no more. We will handle it from here," Bless said hanging up the phone.

He looked over at his two partners and said, "One of you come with me and the other one stay in the car and keep the engine running. As soon as Ed and his crew walks out, we are going to blast their ass," Bless said cocking his 9mm back putting one in the chamber.

* * * *

"Alright, I'm about to bounce," Chan said as he and Wan started to head for the door. "Are you going to be cool with this trouble maker?" he said, as he smiled at Ed.

"Yeah I'm good, but can you make sure you send Denver that new package tomorrow? They will need it for next week," EJ said watching Chan get ready to leave.

"I'm on it in the afternoon when I get up," Chan said giving his friend a pound and rolling out.

"Are you good to drive?" EJ asked Maria who had come by herself.

"Yeah I'm good. I will see y'all next week," she said as she gave him a hug. Before she let him go, she whispered in his ear, "Happy birthday and I want some dick tomorrow so come through."

EJ smiled and got ready to leave with Ed, Tamara, and Yahnise. They all walked out the club together and the cool air instantly hit them. It was a little chilly outside so EJ put his hat on and zipped up his coat. Ed was sobering up from the cool air and the fight earlier. As they started walking towards the car, they didn't noticed the two men getting out of the car across the street.

* * * *

"There they go, right there. Let's get them now," Bless said getting out of the car with his man right behind him. They ran across the street firing wildly.

BOC! BOC! BOC! BOC! POP! POP! POP! POP! POP!

"Oh shit Ed, get down!" EJ yelled while jumping on top of Yahnise as they both fell to the ground.

Ed did the same to Tamara who was screaming hysterically and they hit the ground.

Ed pulled out his 40 caliber that the bouncers let him get in with and started firing in the direction that the shots were coming from.

BOOM! BOOM! BOOM! BOOM!

Gunshots were all that could be heard as the men exchanged gunfire back and forth.

All of a sudden, another gun blazing was heard. POP! POP! POP! POP! POP! It was Maria firing on the men.

The two men retreated backwards firing crazy reckless shots as people started ducking and running. During all of the wild shooting, a bullet struck Maria in her neck.

Ed jumped up and let off on the car that the two men got in as it spent the corner. The whole time EJ had his body shielding Yahnise from harm. He didn't even know that Maria was lying in a pool of blood until Ed screamed her name.

EJ jumped up and ran over to her. She was on the ground gagging for air while her body was twitching and jerking wildly.

"We have to get the fuck out of here now!" Ed yelled trying to pull EJ away.

"We can't leave her like this," EJ said holding her in his arms. He didn't move until Yahnise grabbed him and began pulling him away.

"Come on baby! She's gone! We can't be here when the cops come!"

EJ looked up at her with tears in his eyes. Then he got up and him, Tamara, Ed, and Yahnise jumped in his car and pulled off, spinning wheels.

What started as a perfect birthday party had ended in a blood bath. This was the turning point for EJ. Unbeknownst to them, they had just created a monster that no one ever wanted to see.

CHAPTER 14

Two weeks passed since the club altercation. They all went to Maria's funeral last week, which was packed just as they thought it would be. EJ finally got the whole scoop from Ed about YG and his squad. He was pissed with Ed, but that was his boy so he wasn't going to let him go out like that by himself. In fact, EJ had put a reward out for information leading him to YG and his squad's cribs. He just wanted all of this to be over so he could get back to making money.

They were still handling business, but now he had to ride with his friends and get those men back for killing Maria. He took over as the head of the organization because nobody else was capable of doing it. He let Maria's people take over her crib and all of her money. He moved all of the computer equipment and anything else that was involved in their business to another location.

He rented a house in Southwest Philly strictly for their meetings. It was a two bedroom, single story house with a basement. It was on a quiet block right off of 56th and Elmwood. It was only for business and nothing else.

Ring! Ring! Ring! EJ's cell phone went off. He looked down at the screen and saw that it was Chan. "Hello," he said into the phone while sitting at his computer staring at the screen.

"What's up man? I just got the call from Denver and Shannon. They said that the money is in route and that you can send another package," Chan said.

"Okay, well, you know what to do and I will get up with you later. I have to meet up with this new bank manager in Delaware. If everything goes well, we can pick back up where Maria left off," EJ said, getting his stuff together so he could meet up with Ronald.

Ronald was a bank manager in a large bank in Wilmington, Delaware. He was also a street nigga from Philly that loved money. . He had been doing business with Maria for a year now and now EJ wanted to do business with him. He told EJ that he would meet him at the crib this evening after work.

Ronald was going to give up one thousand account and routing numbers for only ten percent of what the crew received on each transaction.

EJ grabbed his coat and headed for the door. He stopped, went back to the dresser, and grabbed his MAC-11 out of the case. Since the shooting at the club, he had stocked up on about ten different guns. The MAC-11 was his new baby, but he also carried a Desert Eagle in the glove compartment of his car.

After EJ grabbed his gun, he hopped in his car and left out to go catch up with Ronald.

* * * *

Ed was over in West Philly on 39th and Wallace, at a Chinese store getting a Dutch. When he came out of the store, he noticed one of the dudes that had shot at him a couple of weeks ago. He stood next to a car talking to some random chicken head.

He was so deep in his conversation that he didn't even notice Ed walking towards him with a 40 caliber in his hand. When he looked up, all he saw was the flash of the gun before his face and chest began to hurt.

BOOM! BOOM! BOOM! That was the sound of the cannon. The dude fell to the ground and tried crawling away, but Ed was right on him. The girl started screaming and without even thinking twice, Ed put a bullet right between her eyes, silencing her forever. Then he aimed his gun back on the dude that was on the ground and emptied his clip in the man's head and body. When they have his funeral, it will have to be a closed casket. That's if his family could even identify him.

Ed jumped in his car and bounced before the cops could get there. He didn't know it, but the girl that he shot's, sister was looking out of her window the whole time, watching the entire thing. She was the one who called the police and was crying and screaming hysterically, but she was going to tell the police everything that she saw. The only problem was that she didn't have a clue as to who Ed was.

* * * *

Yahnise was on the phone talking to Nyia about everything that had transpired the past couple of days. EJ had told her to find them a bigger house that they could move into after the wedding. Nyia was suggesting that they came out her way.

"Girl I told you to come out here. I know where this beautiful house is on King Street and it has a big pool in the back," Nyia said to her sister.

"Well I will be over your house tomorrow after EJ and I come from the doctor's office. Then we can look at some place on the computer together," Yahnise, said, as she was making dinner.

"Okay, I get off of work at four and I'm coming straight home so I will meet you here," Nyia said.

"Good, because we have to get the rest of the ideas for my wedding from that wedding planner that you used. I just want everything to be perfect. I'm about to finish dinner so I'll see you later," Yahnise said, hanging up the phone.

* * * *

When EJ arrived home at 10:00 that night, Yahnise was upstairs in their bedroom laying on their king sized bed wearing nothing but one of EJ's t-shirts. She was on her stomach, propped up on her elbows watching, "The Bad Girls Club" on TV. She was laughing at how the girls were dancing around the pool when she heard someone coming up the stairs. A couple of seconds later, EJ entered their bedroom. "Hey baby! What are you doing?" he said cheerfully as he gave Yahnise a kiss and then started taking off his clothes.

"Nothing, just watching The Bad Girls Club. I made dinner for you. Are you hungry?" she asked, as she watched him put on some basketball shorts and a wife beater.

"Yeah, I'm hungry, but not for food," EJ said as he came over and sat on the bed and slowly and gently massaged and played with Yahnise's exposed pussy.

"Well damn... I guess she misses you too," Yahnise replied, as she felt her pussy getting wet instantly. After he played with her pussy for a few minutes, she quietly got up and EJ felt Yahnise's warm mouth all over his dick. Yahnise did her best to deep throat EJ's dick as she started kissing and licking the head. She had never sucked anybody's dick before she met EJ. He was her first oral pleasure and hopefully her last. In fact, she really hated sucking dick, but since her and EJ had got together; there wasn't anything she wouldn't do to please him. EJ was enjoying the work his fiancé was putting in as he reached around and slid two fingers inside Yahnise's soaking wet pussy.

"Damn baby... That feels so good," Yahnise moaned with her mouth still full of EJ dick. EJ's fingers felt so good that she could feel herself about to cum on his hand. When EJ heard her breathing speed up and he felt her clit swell, he knew she was about to cum. He quickly pulled his fingers out of her pussy and his dick out of her mouth. He wrapped her legs around his waist as he slide inside her warm walls. Yahnise gyrated her hips pushing her pussy back on his long hard dick as EJ sped up the pace. Their bodies glistened with sweat while they got busy on the bed like two porn stars filming a movie.

"Oh shit! YESSSSSSS! Yes baby! You are fucking the shit out of this pussy," Yahnise yelled in a sexually charged tone of voice. EJ was digging her back out. She was contracting her pussy muscles to clench down tightly on his dick. He was stretching her walls with each long pounding stroke.

"You love when I hit this pussy like this; don't you?" EJ groaned as he continued pounding her pussy like his life depended on it.

"Yes baby! Oh my God! I love this dick. Fuck me baby! Yes! Tear this pussy up! YESSSSSSS! Just like that! I'm about to cummmm," she screamed loudly, while she fucked him back harder and faster to meet his powerful thrusts.

EJ and Yahnise were both moaning and groaning during this intense fuck fest, until Yahnise couldn't hold back any longer. "Yes! Right there baby! OH MY GOD! I'm cummming! I'm cummming!," Yahnise yelled out in ecstasy while biting down on her bottom lip letting the feeling of EJ's dick pounding her pussy take her to another world.

"That's a good girl... Cum for me baby," EJ said aggressively, while not breaking his stride. He was pounding in and out of her gushing wet pussy with a steady rhythm.

"Tell me where you want it baby. Do you want it on your stomach or in your pussy?" EJ asked as he was about to explode also.

"Mmmmm... Keep it in my pussy baby. Please leave it in and don't pull out until you're empty. I wanna feel that shit shooting all up inside of me," Yahnise begged.

After about another minute or so, EJ exploded with a crazy burst of hot semen all up inside of Yahnise's pussy. If she weren't pregnant before, she sure would be now. EJ started shaking real bad and then he fell on top of her.

"Damn girl! I love you so much! I can't wait until July," EJ said, kissing her on the lips. He rolled off of her exhausted. "Now get up and go get my dinner woman," he said picking up the TV remote and turning the channel to watch the Knicks play Miami.

Yahnise got up and EJ smacked her on her ass making it clap. She loved when he did that. "Don't start nothing that you can't finish," she said, as she put on her robe and left the room to go get EJ's dinner.

EJ laid there thinking to himself, what would he do without her in his life... He hoped he would never have to find out.

CHAPTER 15

Agent Kaplin was on the phone with Detective Harris. "You were right. The ID's that they used were fake. We only have faces, but no names to go with them," Agent Kaplin said.

"So where do we go from here?" Detective Harris asked with a little hint of frustration in his voice. He had been trying to crack this case ever since they had put it on his desk. He was relentless and determined to move up in the ranks. Right now, he was back at square one.

"Well, I'm still looking into some things. I think we are going to have a bigger case than we thought. If these people are using fake IDs then that's a federal case for false identification and identity theft. We can add those onto the list of other charges, but we need to be careful so that we don't mess this up. If this case is as big as we think it is, then we can get them for a whole lot more," the agent said as he looked at the paperwork from the bank.

Detective Harris wanted to scream, but he knew that the agent was right so he controlled his anger. "Okay, so are we a team on this and can you get this authorization from your superiors to get this ball rolling?"

"I have a meeting tomorrow morning with my boss about this. I would like you to join me so you can let him know what you have also. Then he will be able to talk with your Commander and make you a part of the task force that I'm sure he will let me form," Agent Kaplin said.

"Well that right there sounds like a plan. What time should I be there?" Detective Harris said sounding all anxious.

"Be here at 9:00 sharp and bring everything that you have on this case even if it's something small. We will be able to convince him better if we have something to go on," Agent Kaplin said.

"I'll be there and I will bring what I can. I know this is something big that we have here and I can't wait to nail them. I'll see you later Keith," Detective Harris said as he hung up the phone.

* * * *

The next morning Detective Harris, Agent Kaplin, and the Bureau Chief were sitting in his office talking about the possible case they had. They had been in there for a little over an hour. After they had explained every detail of the case and their little-to-nothing leads that they had, the Bureau Chief was a little skeptical about giving them the green light on it. In spite of his better judgment, he granted them a thin line to proceed with the investigation.

"I'm not going to give you a great deal of agents on this right now, but I will give you ten to start off with. You can pick anyone you want that's not working on something else right now. If and when you bring me something more concrete, I'll give you more agents," the Bureau Chief said signing the paperwork.

"All surveillance will be very limited right now. I will also not be approving overtime on this until you produce something more incriminating," he said, looking at Detective Harris and Agent Kaplin. "I will be calling your boss and informing him of the same thing I just told the both of you," he said getting up.

They both picked up on the hint that the meeting was over. They got up and walked to the door and then Agent Kaplin turned around and said,

"We won't let you down boss. We are going to get to the bottom of this and nail anyone that has anything to do with it." Then they both exited the office.

"Well we didn't quit get exactly what we wanted, but we sure as hell got enough," Agent Kaplin said, as he and Detective Harris walked over to his desk.

"Now the hard work begins and when we get these motherfuckers; that will give me the credentials I need to move up in the ranks. I know it's more to this than we have here and we will soon find out what it is," Detective Harris said, as they sat down and started looking at the photos together.

They had three photos. The first photo they had was of two females and one male. The second photo they had was of two males, and the third photo was of one female. Detective Harris had a copy of all of their IDs. They were all fake IDs, but at least it was a start of what was yet to come. What they weren't aware of was that these five people that they had pictures of were nothing compared to what they were facing. In fact, they were just a tiny piece to the puzzle because they had over forty people working for them.

"We have to start here and work our way to the top inch by inch," Agent Kaplin said as they started making a board for possibly the biggest scam organization of their careers. They had nothing to go on, but they were convinced that they would have something real soon.

"I'll grab us some coffee and call my wife and let her know that I won't be home until late," Detective Harris said and sighed as he walked over to the coffee table.

"Yeah, I guess I will do the same," Agent Kaplin said.

Two Weeks Later

Agent Kaplin and Detective Harris were at the Federal Credit Union on 50th and Baltimore Avenue talking to the bank manager about some of the checks that were cashed there a couple of months ago.

"Well, like I told you guys, I'm pretty new here. I took over for Ms. Sanchez after she was killed outside of some club. I'm still catching up on all of the files and reports here. Once I do and I get things together, I will give you guys a call," Ronald said, looking at the detective and agent suspiciously. Ronald had taken over a couple of banks that Maria was in charge of when she passed away. He was the new district manager now and he wanted to get away from these guys so he could hurry and call EJ.

"Okay, no problem. We will be back in a week and we hope that if you have any information earlier that you will give us a call," Agent Kaplin said, as they headed for the door.

As they were walking out of the bank, Detective Harris saw a familiar face coming out of the bodega across the street. He stared a little harder and realized that it was one of the people from the photo.

"Yo, look at that girl right there. Doesn't she look familiar?" he said to Agent Kaplin.

Agent Kaplin turned to see what he was talking about as Detective Harris was already flipping through the folder in his hand looking at the pictures.

"Right here! I knew it!" he said showing Agent Kaplin the picture.

"Well we can't do anything to her right now, but let's follow her and see where she lives and then we can go from there." They both rushed to the car and started to follow the girl. She pulled up to a house on 63rd and Callowhill about fifteen minutes later.

They watched as she walked in the house and decided to stake out the place for a while. After about an hour, they wanted to get back to the station to try and find out what they could about that house. "We'll put one of the agents on her and see where it will lead us," Agent Kaplin said, as they started to head back to the headquarters.

This was their first small break in the case and they wanted to make sure that all of their I's were dotted and their T's were crossed before they messed up.

CHAPTER 16

July 4, 2011

Ed was really getting money now. He had turned up his work a little bit more and was now selling loud. He would get a pound for $2,500.00 and make almost $10,000.00 off of it. His connect was giving him the sweetest deal ever. He had upped his coke buy up to keys now. His connect only charged him $26,000.00 a key and if he purchased two, he would get another two on consignment. He was killing the game in more than one way. He had coke, loud, and the check scam.

The problem he was having was that it had gotten too hot in the streets to sell it on the corners so he was giving it up dirt cheap. As long as he paid his connect, he wasn't worried. He was actually losing money by selling weight.

What he really needed was to lock a couple of blocks down and that's what he planned on doing. He promised himself that after EJ's wedding that he was going to take the world by storm. Right now, he was getting ready to go see his best friend take that leap of faith.

"Tamara bring your ass on! I don't want to be late!" Ed yelled up the stairs waiting for Tamara to get dressed. "You now I'm the best man!"

"Well let's go then," she said coming down the steps in a black strapless Channel dress. She looked stunning and Ed wanted to fuck her as soon as he saw her, but he couldn't be late.

They left for the wedding that would be starting in about an hour. This was going to be a big event.

* * * *

Everyone was patiently waiting for the wedding to begin. There was a little over two hundred guest there. The wedding was taking place on the *Spirit of Philadelphia*. It was a ship at Penns Landing. After a lot of convincing, Yahnise had talked EJ into having it there. Everything was decorated beautifully. EJ had hired Ms. Anne, a small business owner to do the catering for the entire event. Her catering company was called, "Our's Catering". It was located in West Philly on Lancaster Avenue. She was renting the building that used to be a Laundromat right off of Preston Street.

Yahnise and her sisters Nyia and Mira were in her room talking and waiting for the ceremony to begin. "Look at my little sister looking so beautiful and ready to walk down that isle," Nyia said holding back tears. She didn't want to mess up her makeup.

"Stop because you are about to make me start crying again," Mira said looking at her sisters. Mira was the youngest out of the three. She was only sixteen, but she was just as beautiful as Yahnise and Nyia. She was bigger than they were and people always thought that she would one day get a scholarship to go to Harvard because she was so smart. Everybody even thought that she would graduate before she turned seventeen.

"I can't believe this day has finally come for me. I just hope that nothing will ever change between us or come between us," Yahnise said nervously.

"Y'all are going to be alright girl. I have never seen anyone else love each other as much as you two do," Nyia said. "Now let's get ready for the show because he has a surprise for you."

"What is it?" Yahnise asked excited because she knew EJ always outdid himself when it came to her.

Mira smiled at her and said, "You will see when the music starts."

They all finished getting ready and then they walked out the door heading for the hall so their sister could marry the love of her life.

* * * *

"Now what we came here to do, it means more to me than just a night, that we'll share so make sure that your prepared baby and know that love..."

Music was coming out of the speakers loudly. The crowd was enchanted by the melody of the music.

"Who knows, somehow, this night, just might lead us into a place where our emotions can grow, if we let em go..."

Musiq Soulchild sang with the live band. EJ had known somebody who knew Musiq's cousin from his old neighborhood. He asked him to sing at their wedding and since he would be in Philly visiting some family members that weekend, he said he would be honored to do it.

Yahnise was walking down the aisle in total shock. She was a beautiful bride. She was wearing a white gown designed by Versace. She knew her husband to be had a surprise, but she didn't expect it to be her favorite singer. This was really the best moment in her entire life and it was all thanks to her man.

Musiq sang until Yahnise was down the aisle and in the arms of EJ. Everyone sat down after the music stopped and the ceremony began.

* * * *

After a night of dancing and having fun at the reception, it was time for the two love birds to go on their honeymoon. Yahnise was due to have her baby next month, but she didn't want that to stop her and her new husband from going on their honeymoon to Jamaica. They would be there for a week soaking up some sun and enjoying each other's company.

Everyone followed them off the boat as they walked to the Hummer limo that awaited them. EJ gave his best friend a hug and said, "Be good until I get back and stay out of trouble."

"I got you bro! You know how I do," Ed said as he winked at his partner. He watched him and Yahnisc as they waved goodbye to everyone and the limo pulled off heading to the airport.

"Well now that they are gone, it's time to get the house ready for when they return," Nyia said to Chris as they got in their car and pulled off.

They told EJ that they would call the moving company and have all of their stuff moved into the new house by the time they got back from their honeymoon. The only thing they didn't have to move was the furniture because EJ had already purchased all new furniture. That made things a lot easier for them because they wouldn't have to make as many trips back and forth.

"Yeah, we have to meet the movers in the morning so let's get home and get some rest," Chris said pulling into traffic.

"Wait, wait, wait a minute," Nyia said looking at Chris. "Why in the morning? If that's the case then we're going to stay at their house tonight. It isn't any reason to drive all the way out to Pottstown and then have to drive back tomorrow."

"That's true so we'll stay out here then," Chris said.

* * * *

Three days later, everything was set up at the new house. Their new house had a master bedroom suite with a beautiful large bathroom. Their bathroom had a large walk-in shower like the ones you would find in the luxury hotel rooms. Their bathroom had marble inside from the ceiling to the floor. Their shower had a RainSpa multi showerhead combination set so the water would hit you from every angle while you showered.

They had a Jacuzzi style tub separate from the shower that was made for two people. There was a patio off of the master bedroom. The entire kitchen was all stainless steel with beautiful granite counter-tops. All of their floors were marble and the kitchen and all of the bathroom floors were heated. The only floors that were not marble were the bedroom floors. All of the bedrooms had thick plush Italian carpet. The basement had a movie room that looked like a miniature movie theater. It was only smaller. It had ten theater chairs. There was a built in bar in the corner and a giant popcorn maker in another corner.

The entire house was fabulous, both inside and out. They had really fixed their house up. It has a three car garage and a gate surrounded the entire property. Nyia even had ADT come out and install cameras in every part of the house so that no one would be able to break in without getting noticed. EJ had paid her good to make sure that everything would be set up and ready for when they returned.

They gave their old house to EJ's God-Sister Theresa. She didn't want to stay in South Philly with her mom anymore so she asked them if she could stay there. EJ loved his God-Sister like a real sister. He would give her anything she asked from him. That's why when she asked if she could stay at their old house when they moved, he immediately said yes.

After everything was set up for them, Nyia and Chris went home. They only lived two blocks away so they could come over whenever they wanted to. "EJ and Yahnise will be home in a couple of days. I really hope they like it," Chris said.

"I know they will. We did a hell of a job baby. Now I want to get some rest before work tomorrow," Nyia said as they headed home.

CHAPTER 17

August 10, 2011

❝Push baby! Push! You can do it. Come on, just a little bit further," EJ said as he held Yahnise hand while she pushed.

They were at Pottstown Memorial Hospital. Yahnise was finally giving birth to their son. They had picked his name just a week ago. They were going with a name that both of them liked. His name was going to be Ziaire.

"Ahhhhh... It hurts baby! It really does!" Yahnise screamed. She didn't want any medication because she was afraid of the side effects so she had natural birth. Boy was she regretting that decision at this very moment.

The doctor said, "One more push and that should do it." Yahnise pushed one more time as hard as she could and sure enough, the baby came out with ease. "That's it. He's out now," the doctor said passing the scissors to EJ so he could cut the umbilical cord.

After EJ cut the cord, the nurse took the baby and cleaned him up. As soon as she had the baby clean, she handed him to his mother so that she could hold him.

All of their family came to the hospital to see little Ziaire. He was a beautiful little boy. He already had some of Yahnise features. EJ was extremely excited about his son. He was truly the proud father.

* * * *

A week later, everyone was back to business as usual. Ed was at his spot out North. He had the whole 29th and Lehigh on smash and his spot on Diamond Street was blowing up. He wasn't taking any losses anymore. "Did you get the package I sent you yesterday?" Ed asked one of his workers. He had sent him a half of brick and he had sent the other half over to Diamond Street.

"Yeah and I'm already offing it. I will have something for you before the night is over," Tuck said. Tuck was one of Ed's newest Lieutenants and probably the best. Ed had hired him about a month ago and he was already doing better numbers than all of his other Lieutenants. Ed was even considering putting him in charge of the entire North Philly while he was taking care of business everywhere else. The only problem with that was he hardly knew him. He had to get to know him a little more before he did that.

"Okay. I'm about to be up out of here. Tamara will be going to see her mom at 8:00. You can drop whatever money you have for me off to her," Ed said before walking out the door. His next stop was Diamond Street so he could meet up with his squad of killers. He was still looking for that nigga YG and now he had one other name as well. It was some killer named Bless.

From what Ed had heard, the nigga Bless was about his work. If somebody wanted to pay someone to get taken out, they called Bless. He was from Delaware and the word on the street was that he would travel anywhere for the right price. He was 5'11 with dreads and he had a tattoo of a scroll on his right arm. People said that before he made his move, he would say the words on the scroll for encouragement.

Whatever the case may be, Ed thought it was now time to turn shit up.

He had a deadly squad of young niggas that didn't give a fuck about anything. Today they were going to destroy one of YG's new blocks. He had a couple of blocks on 25th and Master Street and it was time for them to go.

Ed pulled up to Diamond Street and stepped out of his Charger. He walked into the house and twenty killers were sitting around waiting on him. "What's up niggas? Are y'all ready to do this?" Ed asked as he picked up the AR-15 that was sitting on the table.

They all nodded in agreement and Ed said, "Well let's go handle this. Everybody must go this time. I don't want any fuck ups like before. That's why none of those bitch ass niggas are not with us now," Ed said, heading for the door.

There were three all black work vans outside in the alley. They loaded into the vans and were immediately on their way to handle some business.

* * * *

EJ, Chan, Wan, Denver, and Shannon were all sitting in the house on 56th street. They were talking about the information that Ronald had told them yesterday. "Ronald said that we should start considering going to other places like Canada, Puerto Rico, and shit like that to start building up some more clientele. What do y'all think about that?" he said, waiting for everyone to answer.

"I think that would be a good idea because I could use some sun and fun time to enjoy myself," Denver said smiling.

"If we do expand to other places, there is a lot that can go wrong if we don't come correct," Chan said seriously.

EJ looked at all of them and said, "I agree. That is why if we do decide to do this, I want to put it off for maybe one or two months. That will give us enough time to plan this thing out right. We will need some very loyal people to handle that type of operation. For now, let's get back to this other shit that we already have going on here."

"Okay we have a check for $3,500.00, one for $4,500.00, and four in the amount of $4,000.00 ready to go," Chan said, showing them the checks. "We also have five people to go file W2s. With each W2, if they claim two kids each, they will bring back $5,500.00 easily."

"Who do we have that's ready to take care of this right now? I don't want to delay this any longer," EJ said.

Shannon stood up and said, "I can do two of the checks as long as Ronald clears them for me at the Credit Union and Bank of America."

"I'll take care of the other four," Wan told everyone. "As a matter of fact, if you print up four more, I can get them cashed also. I have four names for you to print on them right now. I'll take them to one bank and then we'll go to the other one," telling Chan.

"Do you have your names as well Shannon?" Chan asked.

"Yes just let me call them and tell them to be ready," Shannon said, taking out her cell phone to call her crew.

"Alright that settles the checks and I will take care of the W2s. I have eight people ready to rock and roll so Chan you can print up three more. Denver you will take four and I will take the other four. We will be working crazy today because it's only us. Ed is nowhere to be found so it's up to us," EJ said as he walked over to Chan as he started printing up the other forms.

Just this one day of work was going to bring them at least $84,000.00, if everything went as planned. Everyone had a job to do so it was time to put in this work. As they all left to go their separate ways, EJ stopped them and said, "Everyone be careful. If you see the first bit of trouble, back down and go. Just remember what Ronald said about those detectives a couple of months ago."

They all nodded their heads, jumped in their cars, and went to pick up their people. EJ took out his phone and tried to call Ed again. After four rings, it went to his voice mail. "Yo, hit me up when you get this. We had an operation today and you're not here to have my back. Let me know that you are good. I'll holla at you," EJ said, hanging up and pulling off in his

Dodge Magnum.

* * * *

An hour later, EJ, and his crew pulled up to the H&R Block on 21st and Oregon Avenue. There was also a Hewitt & Jackson three doors down. "Okay, I'm going to go in with the two of you and y'all can go into the other one," EJ said to the other two girls. He had to go in with the first two because this was their first time doing this. Jaimie was from down the bottom on 39th Street. She was light skin and very beautiful. She had a body like Rihanna, but her ass was a little bigger. Kelly was brown skin with big titties. Her body was a little on the thick side like the old Christina Aguilera, but she was still beautiful. They both were new to this part of the game even though they had both cashed a few checks. EJ wanted to be there just in case they needed him.

When they walked in the door, the place wasn't crowded as it was the last time he was there. They only had to wait for twenty minutes before a lady called the next person on her clipboard.

"Jaimie Dunden," the lady said, looking around for the person whom she had just called.

"Okay, let's do this," Jaimie said, getting up and following the lady to her desk.

"So how can I help you?" the lady asked.

"Yes, I would like to file my income taxes," Jaimie said, as if she had done this a thousand times. Then she passed her paperwork to the lady.

The lady looked over the forms and asked," May I have your state ID please?"

Jaimie passed the lady her ID and the lady began typing away on her keyboard. After a couple of minutes the lady asked, "Do you have any dependents?"

Jaimie gave the lady all three of the children's names that she was using along with their social security numbers. The lady began typing away again. After about thirty minutes, the lady completed all of the configurations.

"Your total refund will be $6,900.00," the lady said.

Jaimie's eyes lit up with excitement. The company that Jaimie was supposed to be working for was Comcast Cable. She claimed her neighbor's twins and her three year old daughter. "That is what's up," Jaimie told the lady.

"We will deduct two hundred dollars for the processing fee. Would you like your money back in three days or ten?" the lady asked Jaimie.

"Three days is good with me," Jaimie said.

The lady typed some more things into her computer, and then told Jaimie, "Your total charges after everything will be three hundred dollars. Your total refund after all fees and taxes have been deducted will be $6,600.00. I will be giving you a Visa check card and the money will be on your card within three business days. I'm going to need you to type in a four digit PIN number twice for your check card." The lady slid the keypad over towards Jaimie. Jaimie typed in a four digit PIN twice and slid the keypad back over towards the lady.

"Okay ma'am, your refund had been processed. If you have any questions or concerns, please feel free to give me a call," the lady said, as she got up from her chair and handed Jaimie one of her business cards along with the Visa check card and all of her paperwork.

Jaimie got up from her seat as well and took the items from the lady. She left the building and went to wait in the car while Kelly did her thing next.

It took about two hours for everyone to finish their tax returns. Everybody had $5,000.00 or more just as Chan had said. After everyone was done, EJ took them to get something to eat and then he dropped everyone off at their homes.

He wanted to visit his aunt Cat so he dropped Jaimie off last. She lived down the street from his aunt.

When he pulled up to the house and parked his car, niggas were on the corner playing basketball with a crate that they had on a pole. EJ remembered those days all too well. "I see nothing has changed around here," he said, as he and Jaimie got out of the car.

"Yeah, you can say that again. I guess I will see you in three days so you can pick up your money," Jaimie said with a smile on her face.

"You might see me before that if you keep on wearing those short ass shorts you got on," EJ said looking at her ass poking out of the bottom of her shorts.

"Whatever! You are a married man now. Wifey will kill you if you stick that little dick in something else," Jaimie said playfully.

"Whoa! Whoa! Who are you talking to like that? First, my dick will tear a hole in that little pussy of yours and second, what my wife doesn't know won't hurt her. You won't tell and I won't either," he said flirting with her.

She laughed as she walked away heading home. When she got to her steps, she turned around and said, "I might think about taking you up on that offer one day." Then she went in her house.

EJ just stood there for a moment smirking. Now that everything was done, he was going to say hello to his aunt and then he would head back to the spot to meet up with everybody else. Before he did anything else though, he called his wife to see how she and the baby were doing.

CHAPTER 18

It had just got dark outside and smokers were all over the place. Ed and his crew had just pulled up to the block. They had been sitting a couple of blocks away for hours waiting for the perfect opportunity to strike. Now that it was dark outside, the time was right.

Ed had told half of his squad to go to the other end of the block while the rest stayed on this side. Everyone was ready to go on his command.

"When I hang up, count to ten and then move out," Ed said to one of his men and then he hung up his cell phone.

After ten seconds went by, all hell broke out on that block. YG's workers never saw it coming. Bodies dropped all over the place. Ed's men had killed everything moving out there, even the smokers.

A couple of niggas tried to get away, but Ed was waiting for them at the corner. As soon as they turned the corner, they were met by Ed's AR-15.

POP! POP! POP! POP! POP! POP! POP! POP!

Their bodies were pumped full of lead. Ed then ran into the stash houses and grabbed the money and work. When they were leaving out, shots rang out from the roof.

BLOC! BLOC! BLOC! BLOC!

BOOM! BOOM! BOOM! BOOM!

Two of YG's goons who were inside one of the stash houses when all the shots rang out arrived. They ran to the roof with an AK-47 and a Riot. Pump. They knew if they had stayed where they were, they were sure to be killed because they outnumbered them by a long shot.

They could have easily gotten away, but they didn't want YG to kill them for not shooting back when his place got robbed. They decided the element of surprise was best so that's when they decided to go to the roof.

Ed jumped back in the stash house as he saw six of his men get hit up. "Get to the roof now and kill them bitch ass niggas!" he shouted, as four men ran for the roof.

Ed's men that were outside took cover and returned fire. When the men got to the roof, YG's men were reloading their weapons. When they looked up, they were met with four guns riddling their bodies.

POP! POP! POP! BOOM! BOOM! BOOM! BLOC! BLOC! BLOC! BOC! BOC! BOC!

The two men died before their bodies even hit the ground. Ed's men retreated as they heard sirens coming. They all ran back to the vans and took off in the opposite direction of the sirens like a thief in the night.

The aftermath of that shootout left twenty-eight bodies sprawled out in a pool of blood. Out of the twenty-eight, twelve of them were innocent bystanders who were in the wrong place at the wrong time. Ed had told them not to leave any witnesses and that's exactly what they did.

* * * *

When they got back to Diamond Street, Ed had three of his men take the vans somewhere and destroy them. He went into the spot to count how much money and work he had taken from the stash house.

"These dumb niggas didn't even keep their shit locked up in a safe," one of Ed's men said as they counted the money and drugs.

"You know that nigga is going to be out for blood now so be careful when you over one of your smuts cribs," one of Ed's workers named Ty said. Ty was a young boy with a lot of knowledge about the streets. At age sixteen, he had lost his brother and mom in a robbery. That alone made his heart cold. The streets had taken his entire family away from him. He didn't care about anything or anybody. That's the reason Ed hired him. He knew that he would put in mad work if necessary.

"Yeah and y'all do the same," Ed said as they finished counting the money. Once they were done counting, they had come up with $27,000.00 and almost a whole key of work. Ed knew YG was going to be pissed off once he found out about that. What Ed really wanted was to bring YG out in the open and face him head-up. He was hoping that this would do just that.

* * * *

"We are live outside of what people are calling the worst massacre in years since the bombings. Twenty-eight people are dead after a violent gun battle tonight. Police have no witnesses, but they are speculating that it was over drugs and territory," the reporter said.

EJ and Yahnise lied in bed watching the news when his cell phone rang. It was Ed so he answered immediately. "Yo, where the fuck have you been?! I've been calling you all day!" EJ said sitting up on the side of his bed.

"Turn on the news and you will see where I have been," Ed said, as he sat on his couch drinking some Hennessy straight from the bottle.

"I'm already watching and don't say anything else on this line. I'll see you tomorrow morning. Don't go anywhere because I'm coming to your crib," EJ said to his friend and then hung up in his ear.

"Who was that baby? Was it Ed?" Yahnise asked, as she starting giving him a shoulder massage.

"Yeah that was him. He is out there getting into trouble again. That's his work right there," EJ said pointing to the TV.

"Damn! He is really going to war out there. I don't want to see you get killed so you need to stay away from him," Yahnise said, wrapping her arms around his neck.

"That's my best friend Yah. If he got beef, then I got beef. He has always been there for me and I will always be there for him," EJ said, standing up and walking around their room.

"Well you have a family now EJ! You have a wife and a fucking son to take care of! What are we going to do if something happens to you? Huh? Tell me that!" Yahnise said, wiping the tears from her eyes.

EJ knew she was right, but he wasn't going to desert his friend. He walked back over to the bed and sat next to Yahnise. "I'm not going to ever leave you or my son. I'm going to have a long talk with him tomorrow. After this is over with, if he doesn't stop this shit, he's on his own. Okay ma," he said, hugging Yahnise.

She looked up at him and nodded her head. EJ passionately kissed her and she got on top of him and began straddling.

He lifted up her night gown and began rubbing her ass as she rocked her pussy back and forth over his hard dick. Just when they were getting into it, their son started crying, hearing him through the monitor.

"Your turn," Yahnise said as she rolled off of him and laid on the bed.

"I got this, but when he goes back to sleep that ass is mine," EJ said, as he got up heading for the door to get Ziaire.

Yahnise threw a pillow at him on his way out the door and said, "I'll be waiting Big Daddy!"

He laughed and went out the door to get his little man.

* * * *

The next morning EJ went to see his best friend. They were sitting in Ed's living room talking about everything that had happened last night. Ed told EJ that he wasn't going to rest until YG was in a grave somewhere or burned to ashes.

"I want this nigga too for what he did to Maria, but to what expense will we have to pay? He's hiding somewhere while someone else is fighting his battles. If something happens to you or someone in our family, niggas is going to bleed and I mean that. I will kill everything moving," EJ said.

"I know I have been going a little crazy out here, but I can't rest until this is done and over with. So will you help me? After this, you have my word that I'll slow down with everything and get this money with you," Ed said looking at his friend. "But you have to incorporate my drug game in with your business. You can take this to a whole new level. You lead and I will follow."

"I don't want you to follow. I want you to be my partner like we always have been," EJ said to his friend.

"So does that mean that we have a deal?" Ed asked, looking at EJ.

EJ thought about it for a minute and then he shook Ed's hand and said, "Deal!"

* * * *

Over on 19th and Erie, YG, Bless, and another dude named Romeo were sitting in the living room smoking loud and drinking Cîroc while discussing their next move. They were watching the aftermath of the killing spree last night.

"So you mean to tell me that nobody survived in our crew and only six of his men checked out (died)," YG said as he puffed on the Dutch.

Bless put his drink down and looked at his boss. "Yeah I guess you can say that. I'm going to handle this personally so there will be no more slip ups. That is why I have my man right here from Delaware with me," he said, dapping up Romeo who was sitting in silence.

"Well I'm going to let you two handle things. Do you need any men because I can hire someone to help?" YG asked them.

"No. We will do this by ourselves. That way, if we don't get them, then you can cancel our contracts permanently," Romeo said, speaking for the first time.

Romeo lived in Wilmington. He was one of the most feared stickup boys out in Wilmington. He was wanted by the FBI for four murders he had committed last year. He had been hiding out in Atlanta ever since then. That is until Bless called him and told him that his services were needed. Now here he was, ready to ride with his boy.

"How long will it take for him to end up on the 11:00 news," YG asked no one in particular.

"I don't work like that my man. You have to give me some time, but it won't take me long, that I can assure you. Don't worry about it. No matter how long it takes me, my price won't change," Romeo said.

"It ain't even about the money. I just want this nigga gone in a hurry. I need to get my money and he is stopping me from doing that," he said.

They sat and talked for another two hours about everything. When Bless and Romeo left YG's house, they knew exactly what they had to do and you could best believe that they were going to get it done.

* * * *

Detective Harris and Agent Kaplin finally had some names to go with the faces on the photos. They had ran them through every database and came up with nothing until they finally got a lucky break. The girls house that they had surveillance on had finally paid off. It belonged to a lady by the name of Cynthia Young who was the mother of a Mr. Edward Young. She had rented the house out to one of Ed's girls who he came over to see when he needed some quick pussy.

Ed's mom never knew that he was also stashing shit there. The detective and agent wanted to talk to this girl named Neicy. They wanted to see what they could get out of her. They didn't know who Edward was because he didn't have a criminal background. The only reason they even had his name was because it was on the tax papers along with his moms.

They pulled up to the house on 63rd and Collowhill. They were going to try to use the fake ID to get to the truth. When they knocked on the door, no one answered.

They knocked again and then they heard the door opening up.

"Yes? Can I help you?" a girl, who couldn't have been any more than fifteen, said.

Agent Kaplin was the first one to speak. "I'm Agent Kaplin and this is my friend Detective Harris," he said flashing his badge while Detective Harris did the same. "We would like to speak to Ms. Neicy Turner."

The whole time that Neicy's cousin Zarina was talking to the police, she was in the bathroom flushing drugs down the toilet. She saw the two officers coming and she got nervous thinking they were raiding her crib.

"She's not here right now, but I will tell her that you came by," Zarina said, trying to close the door.

Agent Kaplin put his foot in the door. "Wait a minute please. Who else is here with you?" he questioned, while trying to peek inside the house.

"Nobody else is here. My cousin is on her way home now so can you move your foot so that I can shut the door please," she said, trying to not let them in the building.

Neicy was now trying to hide the gun that Ed had left there. She accidentally dropped it and when it fell and hit the floor, it went off because, for some reason, the safety wasn't on.

BOOM!

The agent and detective heard the shot and immediately drew their weapons as they rushed in the door. They started searching the house when they spotted Neicy trying to run out of the back.

"FREEZE! Federal Agent!" Agent Kaplin said, pointing his gun at Neicy.

Detective Harris had Zarina with him as they watched Agent Kaplin started putting the cuffs on Neicy.

"Why were you trying to run and where is the gun that you just fired?" he said, setting Neicy down in a chair.

"I didn't mean for it to go off. I just got scared; that's all," Neicy said, as she started crying.

"Why were you flushing drugs down the toilet?" Detective Harris asked as he came out of the bathroom with empty bags that had coke residue still in them.

"I thought you were coming to raid the place," Neicy said giving up a confession without being pressured.

"Well it seems like we have a lot to talk about so you can either do it here or down at the station," Detective Harris said, taking a seat.

Without even second guessing it, Neicy started talking to the agent and detective. She told them all about Ed and his mom. She also told them how she got the fake ID and how she had been cashing checks for Ed. She said that by doing that, they had let her stay in the house and she only had to pay half of the rent.

The agent and detective quietly listened as she continued talking. They asked questions and took notes. When it was all said and done, they were smiling from ear to ear as they glanced at each other with approval. They had finally got what they needed to proceed with this case. The only question now was; how can they get everybody at one time? This was going to take some time, but now it was finally starting to fall into place.

CHAPTER 19

Ed was on his way out to West Philly to pick up some money from one of his workers on 42nd and Pennsgrove when his cell phone started to ring. He looked down at his phone and saw that it was Neicy calling him.

"What's popping baby girl?" he said into the phone.

"I really need to talk to you when you get the time. Something happened and I had to get rid of the work," she said sounding nervous.

Ed pulled his car over because he was pissed off about losing two keys of raw.

"What do you mean you had to get rid of the work? What happened?" he asked, trying to control his anger.

"The cops came here and they were looking for me, but they never said why. Then I tried to hide the stuff because I thought it was a raid. When I tried to hide the gun, it fell to the floor and went off," she said trying to give him the full story. Next thing I knew, there was a gun pointed at me, and someone was yelling for me to freeze. They started asking me questions, but I didn't tell them anything," she lied.

"I'll send my mom over there later. Just stay there and don't let anyone in. I have to figure out something," Ed said as he hung up the phone.

What he was really thinking was why in the hell is she not in jail if she didn't say anything... That alone confused him. Either she told on him or she is lying so she could keep the work and give it to somebody else. She had never tried anything before which made him think that she had snitched so she wouldn't go down. Now he had to take care of her before the cops could get any more information out of her.

Ed picked his cell phone up and called Tuck. He answered after a couple of rings. "Yo, what's up Ed? I'll be ready for you by tonight," he said before Ed could get a word out.

"I'm not calling about that right now. I need you to handle something for me," Ed said.

"Whatever you need just let me know and I got you," Tuck said sensing something was up with him.

"I need you to go over to 63rd and Collowhill and take care of what's inside. Make sure that you are not seen by anyone. The spare key is under the flower pot that sits on the porch. Once you are done, destroy everything and call me," Ed said trying not to be conspicuous about it.

"I'm on it and I'll see you later," Tuck said, ending the call.

Ed pulled back out into traffic heading for his spot so that he could finish making his rounds.

* * * *

Chan and Ed were at the office on 56th Street. They were working on their next mission which was to get some checks over to Canada and Puerto Rico. They both knew that this was going to set them over the top if all went well so they had to be on point.

"You did a damn good job on these," EJ said looking at the checks. They were all worth $80,000.00 apiece.

The plan was to take them over to Canada and set up an account. Once they had set up the account, then they would deposit the checks. What concerned them the most was they didn't want to deposit them too quickly. With that being said, EJ decided that they should set the accounts up on-line and then wait for thirty days before they deposited any checks into the account.

"Yeah and now all we have to do is wait for the right time to deposit the checks. While we are waiting for that time to lapse, you can be setting up some more accounts," Chan said to his partner.

"I'm on it now. I just have to figure out whom I'm going to send over there. I was thinking about Denver and Tiffany for this run and then on the next one, we'll send about six different people. That of course all depends on how this goes," EJ said, as he sat down at the computer and begin filling out bank information for Tiffany and Denver.

They were two of his best workers, which is why he always gave them first pick on the jobs that made the most money.

After he set up the accounts in their names, he decided to do the same for him and Ed. He logged onto the Cayman Islands bank web-site and started filling out the information to set up the account.

EJ and his wife had a joint account with Bank of America. His other bank account was with Beneficial Bank and that was a single account. In his Beneficial Bank account, he had over $300,000.00. He saved that money just in case anything went wrong. He wanted to have money for a lawyer on deck. In his joint account, they had a little over $300,000.00. He told Ed that he wanted to reach a million dollars before he turned thirty and he was well on his way. He was only twenty-one years old and he was already past the half way mark. Ed had split his drug money with him so that's why he had such a big savings. They were killing the game on both ends. They had this drug and check thing on lock.

EJ transferred $100,000.00 from his Beneficial Bank account over to his new Cayman Islands Bank account. He wanted that account to reach the million dollar mark. That was his goal. His local accounts were going to continue to grow also especially with all of the drug money coming in.

He figured if he would send all of the drug money that he made overseas and keep all of the money he made from the checks in his bank accounts here then he would be all right.

"Well that's done so now all we have to do is get ready to go over there in about a month," EJ said, looking at Chan who was busy making more checks.

"Alright that's cool. I'm about to leave so that I can give everyone their packages," Chan said as he shook EJ's hand and headed for the door.

"You be careful on your journey. I'm going to go and see what's up with Ronald. He should have the new numbers for me by now. We can't use those other ones anymore. We have burnt them out; don't you think?" EJ said to Chan.

"Yeah, we have used every last one of them twice and we really should have only used them one time. As long as nobody gets caught up, we should be cool. I'm deleting all of the numbers when I get back," Chan said.

EJ was about to let him leave when he remembered something. "Oh, and we have ten people that need driver's license by the end of the week. I told them that it would cost them $3,000.00 a piece and that comes with a new social security card and a birth certificate. Is that cool?" he said to Chan.

"Yeah that's cool. I just have to stop and see Angie for some more paperwork," Chan said walking out of the door.

Angie worked at the DMV downtown. She would provide Chan with names temporary papers to get social security cards and birth certificates. Then she would give him the card stock to make the licenses for the people. She would get thirty percent of whatever they made off of each sale. She wasn't greedy. She just wanted to make some extra money on the side. It all worked out for all parties involved and everything was going smoothly.

The driver's licenses that Chan made were legit. If someone was ever pulled over, all that they had to do was give the officer the fake license. When the officer would run the fake license, it would come back showing that person's name and picture. They had already tested a few of them.

EJ finished his work, and left so he could pick up his son from

Yahnise's moms house. Ms. Pam would watch Ziaire whenever they needed her to. She would try to keep all of her grandkids as much as possible. If it was up to her, she would never let them go home. That would never happen with Ziaire though. EJ loved Ziaire more than life itself.

Tomorrow was Sunday and he was taking Yahnise and Ziaire to take pictures tomorrow. Sunday was considered family day and they tried to spend every single Sunday together as a family. They had been doing this since Ziaire was born. So far, they had not missed a Sunday yet.

When EJ came out of the house, he saw one of the chicks that he used to mess with a long time ago named Lisa. Lisa was light skin, thin with a nice ass, and some nice size titties. She was walking down the street with her sister Loraine. EJ stood there for a minute until she finally noticed him and walked over to where he was standing.

"Hey EJ. What are you doing down here?" she asked, giving him a hug.

"I was just leaving to go pick up my son. What are you doing down here?" EJ asked while looking at the tattoo she had on her chest that said "EJ." She had gotten that when they were together. EJ didn't want any tattoos because he didn't like needles.

"Well my sister and I just moved down here in April. We live on Alter Street. Wait a minute. Did you just say that you are going to pick up your son? When did you have a baby and who is he by?" Lisa said, looking like she now had a slight attitude.

"Yeah I said my son and he was born last August. I've gotten married and everything. Our wedding was on July 4th," EJ said, pulling out his wallet to show Lisa some pictures of his family.

"Wowwww! I guess I'm lunching, huh… I see you got yourself a nice little family and all," Lisa said looking irritated.

EJ hit the automatic starter on his Magnum and Lisa couldn't believe that this nigga had really come up. She had been hearing all about him from people that knew both of them, but to see it for her own eyes made her panties wet. She still wanted him, but now that she knew he was married, she knew she didn't have a chance.

"Well it was nice seeing you again Lisa. Can I get your number so that I can hit you up and check on you sometime?" EJ asked as he took his cell phone out.

Lisa gladly put her number in EJ's cell phone. The whole time she was thinking that if he ever called her, she was going to try to fuck her way back into his life. After they exchanged numbers, EJ gave her another hug and she made sure to press her body hard up against his to see if she could feel an erection. After that, she walked back over to where her sister was waiting for her and she put a little extra switch in her walk because she knew EJ would be watching.

"*Damn! She has got a little thicker since the last time I saw her,*" EJ thought to himself as he got in his car and pulled off.

* * * *

Ed was in Delaware fucking one of his chicks named Taneesha when his phone rang. He stopped in mid-stride and looked over at the caller ID. His connect that lived over on 24th and Jefferson. That was only a couple of blocks away from where he was right now.

"Yeah," he said into the phone as he started back fucking Taneesha. He was fucking her from the back with one hand holding his phone and his other hand on her lower back.

"I'm ready for you. Come on through and hurry up so I can get back to what I was doing," he said and hung up the phone.

Ed had called him over two hours ago to meet up, but he was busy. He told Ed that he would call him when he was ready. Ed decided to go visit one of his jump-offs while he waited for his connect to get back with him. As soon as he started digging her back out, he got the call.

"Damn Ma, I have to go," he said as he began pumping faster.

"Not before I get my nut," Taneesha said as she started throwing her pussy back harder. She was really getting into it until Ed just stopped and started to pull his shorts up. "Where are you going Ed?! You're a fucking asshole for this!" she screamed with venom in her voice.

"I'll talk to you later. This business can't wait any longer. My peoples are waiting for me. If you just chill the fuck out, I'll come back later tonight and take care of you," Ed said as he walked out the door.

The new connect that he had been dealing with had some good shit. That was the only reason he dealt with him. He wanted to go on his own so as soon as his connect would let him meet his supplier, he was going to cut all ties with him. In addition, he really didn't trust this new guy that much anyway. Work around the hood was that he would sell you weight and then try to rob you for it later.

That's why Ed had a couple of niggas from Delaware on deck for when he came to see him. They would be watching from a window with two Sniper Riffles waiting for the first sign of trouble. So far, he had not tried anything. Ed was going to get the work and head back to Philly. He had money to make and that's what he intended to do. He also had to go over Jersey to pay his weed man a visit. He wanted a half pound of Loud (weed) and he told him that he would be over there after he came from Delaware. First, he was going to stop at home and switch cars. Then he would go back to Philly and chill for the rest of the evening while getting money.

CHAPTER 20

Detective Harris left from the courthouse on 13th and Filbert from getting a warrant to tap Ed's cell phone. He wanted to find out everything he could on him, and find out who was supplying him with the fake checks and IDs. He thought he was close to breaking this case wide open. Now he was on his way to catch up with Agent Kaplin who was watching the house on 63rd Street waiting for Ed or his mom to come by and collect some money from Neicy. As he was driving, he decided to call in a favor from one of his Crime Scene Investigation (CSI) buddies.

From that one phone call, he found out that Ed had something to do with a shooting that occurred about a year and a half ago. He wanted to see if the forensics from the crime scene matched any of the forensics that they had received from the house.

"CSI Office, Officer Myers speaking. How may I help you?" Kathy said, as she continued to work while answering the phone.

"Hey Kathy, this is John. I was wondering if the forensics had come back yet on that murder scene from down on 39th and Wallace," he asked, watching traffic.

"Why are you worried about that? You're not homicide, John. What are you up to now?"

"I'm not up to anything. I'm trying to crack another case that may be similar to or tied to your case," Detective Harris said, hoping that she would take the bait.

"Well if what you are saying is true, then you might as well keep looking because that case is at a stalemate right now. We are no further from solving that case than the one about the twenty-eight bodies found in North Philly. There was no witnesses, no evidence, and no nothing. The shooter got away Scott free. Even the girl that witnessed the shooting on 39th Street can't give a good enough description to help us with a lead on that case. I wish someone would come forward with something useful," she said sighing.

"Well if you get anything for me, please give me a call. If you get something for me, I will take you to dinner for it," Detective Harris said, then hanging up.

* * * *

Ed was driving down Route 38 on his way back to Philly. He had stopped at Cherry Hill Mall to get something to wear at the club that night. As he was driving, he noticed that a State Trooper was following him. He didn't have his gun on him because he had Tamara's car, but he did have a ½ pound of weed in the car with him. At this point, it was nothing he could do so he just kept on driving being sure not to go over the speed limit hoping that the trooper didn't pull him over.

As soon as he thought he was in the clear, the State Trooper hit his siren.

"SHIT! FUCK!" Ed yelled as he put on his signal light to pull over.

Once he pulled over to the shoulder, two State Troopers got out of the car and walked towards his car; one on each side. They both had their hands on their weapons as they approached his car.

Ed had a look on his face as if he had just shit himself. He was trying to keep his composure because he didn't want to alarm them. It didn't help that he was also a little high from smoking some weed earlier. He rolled his window down and waited.

"Hi, how are you doing sir? Can I please see your license, registration, and insurance card, please?" the trooper said.

Ed reached in the glove compartment and grabbed all of his paperwork. Then he reached in his pocket, pulled out his license, and gave everything to the Trooper that was on his side of the car. "What am I being pulled over for," Ed asked, after handing the Trooper his paperwork.

"You have a taillight out in the back," the Trooper said. "Sit tight and we will be right back."

Both men walked back to their car to run Ed's information. He knew nothing would come back on him because he had paid all of his tickets and he had never been arrested before so he wasn't worried about any outstanding warrants.

After about five minutes of waiting, another State Trooper's car pulled up. When the State Trooper got out of his car, Ed noticed that he went to the back of his car and opened the back passenger door. The Trooper was letting out his K9. Along with the other two officers, they all walked back to Ed's car.

"Can you please step out of the car, sir?" one of the Troopers asked.

"What is going on now? I didn't do anything officer," Ed said, while stepping out of his car hoping and praying that they didn't find the loud he had stashed in the back under the seat.

"We thought we smelled Marijuana so we asked for a K9 to come to make sure you didn't have any in your car. If everything goes well, you will be on your way in about ten minutes," the trooper said.

They told Ed to sit on the ground behind his car while the K9 searched his car. Ed was thinking that he wished he had run when he had the chance.

The K9 started barking as soon as he got in the backseat of Ed's car. The troopers immediately started to search his car. One of the troopers pulled out the green bag and that's when Ed really almost shit his pants.

"Damn! What the fuck! I can't even say it's Tamara's because I can't let my wife go to jail! I'm fucked! I just might as well face it," he said to

himself as the troopers started walking towards the back of the car where he was sitting.

"Stand up please and put your hands on the top of your head and face the car. You are under arrest for possession of marijuana with the intent to distribute. You have the right to remain silent. Anything you say, can and will be used against you in a court of law. You have the right to an attorney. If you cannot afford an attorney, one will be provided for you. Do you understand the rights that I have just read to you? With these rights in mind, do you wish to speak to me?" the Trooper said, reading Ed his Miranda Rights while placing the cuffs on him.

Ed didn't say a word. One of the Troopers escorted him to the back of the squad car and they transported him to Camden County Prison. The whole time he was in the car, he was thinking to himself, "*I have to call EJ to get me out of this mess.*"

* * * *

EJ and Jamie were on their way to take care of a few more checks. He had just processed four more for the day. The whole crew had really been grinding hard these past few weeks. In total, they had made approximately $600,000.00.

"Once you cash these last four out in New Jersey, we will chill for a week so you and everybody else can enjoy some of that hard earned money," EJ said, while driving over the Ben Franklin Bridge.

"I know that's right. I'm going on a big ass shopping spree with my sister," Jamie said.

"How is Trina doing with her new job? I haven't seen her around lately," EJ said, while looking at the traffic.

Jamie looked over at him and said, "She's doing well. She is just working hard as hell at that hospital."

Trina was a registered nurse (RN) the University of Pennsylvania. She was studying to become an X-ray Technician. She was engaged to some dude named Brad. They had been engaged for two years now and they still hadn't set a date for the wedding. People were starting to think that they were never going to get married.

"That's good. Tell her I said hello when you talk to her again," EJ said.

Fifteen minutes later, they pulled up to the bank. Jamie went in and did her thing. She went into the bank to cash one check and then she walked around to the ATM and deposited another check in her account.

When they were done there, they went to another bank and did the exact same thing. The checks that she cashed were only for $1,700.00, but the checks that she deposited into the ATM were for $65,000.00 and $78,000.00. Both of the checks were from an insurance scam that they had put together about a month ago. Altogether, this one lick would land them around $146,000.00.

That was good for one person. Jamie had really been handling her business lately. She wanted in on everything, and didn't have a problem with doing anything that EJ asked of her. That's why she was one of his top paid workers now.

Just as they were pulling off to head back to Philly, EJ received a phone call. He didn't recognize the New Jersey phone number so he was a little skeptical about answering the call, especially since they had just left the different banks.

"Hello," he answered anyway wondering who this could be.

"EJ this is Ed. I got locked up and I'm waiting to see a judge for bail," Ed said sounding frustrated.

"What the fuck did you get locked up for? Where are you? I'll be there to get you out as soon as you tell me where you are. I'll call Savino also to make sure your bail hearing goes right," EJ said, with nervousness in his voice. He didn't know what had happened, but he was already scared for his friend.

"I'm at Camden County and they said I won't be able to see a judge until later on tonight. I will call you as soon as I do. Call Tamara and let her know what happened to me," Ed said.

"I got you bro. I'm in Camden now so I will just stay out here until I hear back from you. I'm going to call Savino and Tamara as soon as I hang up. Don't worry about anything. I'm going to get you out," EJ said to his friend.

"Okay nigga. I will fill you in on everything when I get out of here. I'll holla at you later," Ed said before hanging up.

"What happened to Ed?" Jamie asked, genuinely concerned.

"He got snatched up, but he didn't say why. We are going to hang out in this area until he calls me back so that I will be close by. Is that okay with you?" EJ said, as they both looked at each other.

"Yes that's okay with me. Just let me know if it is anything that I can do to help," Jamie said.

"I have to call my wife and Tamara to let them know what is going on. Then I'm going to call Louis Savino, our lawyer so that he can do his job and get Ed out of that hellhole."

* * * *

Two hours had passed and they still had not heard back from Ed. That could only mean that he had not got a chance to see a judge yet. EJ had talked to his wife and Tamara and they both said that they would be waiting by the phone to see what happened. EJ didn't tell them that Jamie was with him. If he had mentioned that small detail, Yahnise would have had a fit.

EJ decided to go over to a hotel until he heard back from his friend since he and Jamie both were kind of tired. Instead of getting two rooms, he just got one. He didn't think that they would be there that long so why waste money on two rooms.

Jamie was lying on the bed while EJ was sitting in a chair watching TV. She got up and went to the bathroom. EJ dosed off while he was watching TV.

He was awakened by someone rubbing on his dick. When he opened his eyes, he saw Jamie on her knees with nothing on but a pair of boy shorts and a bra. EJ's eyes got wide as hell when he saw Jamie's perfect body.

"What are you doing girl? This is not the time for this," EJ said, never taking his eyes off of her beautiful titties.

"I told you that I would have to take you up on that offer one day. Now since we are here with nothing else to do, I think this is the perfect time," she said as she took his now erect dick out of his pants and started stroking it with her hands.

"Well damn! Well go ahead and handle your business then," EJ said while watching her put his dick in her mouth.

After about five minutes of Jamie sucking on his dick, EJ stopped her and led her over to the bed. At first, they just laid there kissing as EJ reached over, stuck his hand in her panties, and started to gently rub on her clitoris.

"Mmmmmm... Ssssss...." Jamie moaned with her eyes closed as EJ looked at the ecstasy all over her face from his finger movement.

EJ then took off her panties and bra. Her nakedness was a perfect work of art and her body looked like it should be on display somewhere.

EJ began taking off all of his clothes and then he got on top of Jamie. He began to rub his dick up and down her wet slit making contact with her clit on each stroke.

"Tell me you want it baby," he said in a whisper, as his dick spasm sporadically a few times against her slippery wet opening.

"Mmmmm... Yes Daddy! Give me that dick! I want it! Please stop teasing me," she moaned as he slowly slid deep inside her wet pussy raw with one long stoke.

"Oh shit!" EJ groaned as he entered her again after pulling out. He could feel her pussy contracting with each trust. It was if her pussy was happy to accept his dick.

Jamie was moaning with her eyes shut. "Yes baby.. Oh my God," she cried out after feeling his dick stretching her walls.

"Yes EJ! Yes baby! Fuck me harder," she shrieked and he continued to pound away at her pussy.

Performing different strokes from circular motions to straight penetration, EJ kept his pace nice and steady. This good dick action was forcing Jamie to bite down on his shoulder as she came all over his dick.

"EJ, EJ, EJJJJJJJ, I'm cumming," she said as her fluids gushed out all over his dick. EJ smiled, but he didn't miss a stride.

As soon as he felt her muscles tighten, he knew she was near a second climax. He turned her over onto her stomach so that he could hit it from the back. Jamie was really enjoying this whole sexual encounter.

EJ's sex game was on point. He never bragged, but his sex game usually turned most women out. Just like any other youngster, when he first started out, his sex game wasn't good at all. Then he fucked some old head and she gave him the experience of a life time. He became familiar with a woman's body. She taught him how to find a woman's sensitive areas and what to do once he found them. Once he learned that, he just used those same techniques on all women and he would always have them climbing the walls before he was done.

He stayed buried deep in Jamie's pussy until it clinched onto his dick. That's when he jammed his dick inside her pussy hard and fast. He went deeper than before to enhance her orgasm.

Jamie's pussy had to adjust to his huge dick before he went at it like a machine.

"Oh shit baby! Here it goes again," Jamie screamed out in total passion, as she climaxed on EJ's dick again.

EJ was almost there too, but he was trying to hold back because her pussy was so good. After a few more strokes, EJ groaned, as he pulled out of her pussy and exploded all over Jamie's beautiful ass cheeks.

Jamie turned over and lay on her back as EJ laid next to her. They both fell asleep for a quick nap still waiting on call from Ed.

* * * *

Around 2:00 a.m., EJ's phone started going off. He thought it was his wife so he jumped up to answer it.

"Hello," he said.

"Hey EJ, this is Savino and I just got Ed a bail for $55,000.00. Bring the money over here now so we can get him out. You only need 10% of that amount," Savino told him.

"I'm on my way there right now," EJ said, putting his shorts on and waking Jamie up so that she could get dressed.

"I'll go get some coffee and sit here and wait for you. Don't be taking all day to get here either. I still have to get some sleep before my golf game later on today," Savino said, joking with EJ.

"I'm only ten minutes away so it's not going to take me long at all. By the time you get your coffee, I'll be there," EJ said before hanging up.

EJ couldn't help; but notice how good Jamie looked, as she got dressed. If he weren't married to Yahnise, he would probably make Jamie his girl. Yahnise was his life so that thought quickly evaporated as they both headed out the door to get his partner out of jail.

* * * *

Later that day, Detective Harris received a phone call from a New Jersey State Trooper. He informed him that they had locked an Edward Young up yesterday and that he had a half pound of marijuana on him. They didn't know that he had made bail already so when Detective Harris called the jail to tell them that he wanted to talk with Edward, they informed him that he was no longer in their custody. He was furious!

He wanted to question Edward about the checks and the fake IDs that he had given Neicy. He didn't have an address for Edward except for his moms address so he decided to pay her a visit.

When he pulled up on 67th and Paschall, he noticed how nice the house was. She had remodeled the whole house on the outside. He knew from the look of things, his mom must have known about his illegal activities. He got out, walked right up to the door, and rang the doorbell.

When Cynthia came to the door, Detective Harris noticed how beautiful she looked. She looked not a day older than twenty-five. "Hello, I'm Detective Harris and I would like to talk to you about your son Edward Young," he said flashing his badge.

"Do you have a warrant because if you don't, you will need to come back when you do," Cynthia said, standing her ground.

"Ms. Young I know what type of business your son is into and I also know that you know all about it. It would be in your best interest to speak with me now or this is all going to go against you later," he said with a warning.

This was his first time seeing her even though they had people staking out her other house on 63rd and Callowhill. He wanted to catch her picking the money up from there because that would implicate her, but that never happened. Right now, he was just hoping that she would at least talk to him so he could pick her brain. She wasn't having any of that though so he had to chalk it up for now.

Cynthia looked at him as if he was crazy. "Like I told you before, if you don't have a warrant then this conversation is over. Have a nice day, whatever you said your name was," Cynthia said as she closed the door in his face.

Detective Harris walked back to his car, turned around, and looked back at the house. "I'm going to get you and your son. You just wait and see," he said out loud to no one in particular, before getting in his car and pulling off.

CHAPTER 21

B less and Romeo had been following Ed's sister for about a week. They were hoping that she would lead them to him. They were tired of waiting for him to come out so they decided to kidnap Erica and that would force him to come out. Just as they were about to run up in the house and snatch her up, Bless thought of another idea.

"I'm going to try and get close to her and once I do, then we can get that nigga," Bless said passing the Dutch to Romeo.

"You think she is going to fuck you?" Romeo asked with a smirk on his face. He could tell that Bless liked Erica because the whole time they were watching her, he was *really* watching her. They had come to know that she really liked money so they would use that as bait to lure her.

"I'm just going to see where her head is and hopefully I'll have her by the end of the week," Bless said, as he got out of the car and followed Erica into the store.

Bless watched her as she ordered her food and drink. He waited until she was about to pay for her stuff and he approached the counter. "Let me get that for you beautiful," Bless said, pulling out a knot of money.

Erica's eyes lit up at the sight of the bankroll. She was used to getting money from her brother and mom, but she also liked for niggas to buy her stuff too. "Thank you, but you don't have to do that," she said.

"Anything for a pretty woman like you. Where is your man? Why isn't he in here with you or better yet, why is he not in here paying for your stuff?" Bless said, looking at the tight shirt Erica had on with no bra.

"That would be nice if I had one, but unfortunately I don't. Where is your woman at?" Erica said, staring at Bless' dreads.

"I don't have one of those either so I guess that makes the both of us single. So that means we can do whatever we want, huh?" Bless said.

Erica looked at him seductively and said, "Well I guess it does."

They exchanged numbers and they both left the store. Bless got back in the car and told Romeo, "I got her man! We are going out tonight and I'm going to tear that ass up and get close to her family. Once I do that, her brother is going to die a slow miserable death,"

"That's the plan then," Romeo said as they pulled off heading back to their crib to just chill out.

Bless couldn't help but think about all of the shit he was going to do to Erica when he got her in the bed. Her fat ass had him mesmerized. *"Soon I will be digging her back out,"* he thought to himself.

* * * *

EJ and Ed were at the meeting house, talking about the overseas accounts that they had. It had been a week since Ed had been home so he had left his boy Tuck in charge of his operation. Tuck had really gained Ed's trust after he took care of that situation on Callowhill Street. Even with the detectives watching the crib, he managed to handle everything. After a couple of days without seeing any movement, they went over to knock on the door. When they didn't get an answer, so they picked the locks and went in. Neicy was gone without a trace. The officers left out of the house in a hurry to put an All-Points Bulletin (APB) out on her. Little did they know she wasn't going to turn up anywhere.

"So did you try to access your account yet?" EJ asked Ed. He had told him about his new account that he had set up for him. This account was for Ed to save money.

"Yeah and that was a good idea that you had the other day. I hope we can also start a couple of trips to Canada," Ed said to his friend.

"You are not going with us, not with your court hearing coming up. I would never let you put yourself in a situation that would make you a fugitive. You have to make that court date. We can handle everything over there while you handle your stuff here," EJ said.

He looked at Ed who was about to say something to object and said, "Trust me Ed. I have a plan and as long as everything goes right, we will be millionaires by the age of thirty. So just trust me on this one, okay?"

"You know I trust you with my life bro, so if that's what you want, then that's what it is," Ed said, while pouring himself a shot of Cîroc.

"We will be leaving for Canada on Sunday. That way we will be back by the end of the week," EJ said.

"Okay, I will handle the normal business here while you are gone," Ed said, as he logged into his Cayman Island account again. He had $400,000.00 in his account already.

"Man I sure hope this all works out like we planned," EJ said, as he and Ed stared at the computer screen.

* * * *

Sunday morning, EJ, Denver, and Tiffany were on a plane heading to Canada. They had work to do and that's just what they intended to do. When they got there, they would get a hotel room and relax until it was almost time for the bank to close. When it was close to closing time, they would go to the bank and deposit some checks. It was a simple operation and they were well prepared for this job. They would deposit the first two checks today and then they would deposit two more checks tomorrow morning.

It was 12:00 p.m. when they arrived in Canada. The weather was nice, so after they got settled in; they decided to go out and enjoy the city. EJ rented a convertible BMW for them to cruise around in. While the ladies went shopping, he stayed at the hotel and called his wife and son.

"Hey baby! How was your trip?" Yahnise said into the phone, while feeding Ziaire.

"We made it here safe and sound, that's all I can say so far," EJ said, laying on the big king size bed. "What is my little man doing?"

"He is eating with his greedy self. Where are the girls at?" Yahnise asked. She wasn't worried about Denver and Tiffany because they were like family along with Shannon. She was only a little worried when he went out of town with everybody else.

"They are out shopping as usual. They better be back here before 3:00 so we can handle this work," EJ said seriously.

"Shut up and leave my friends alone. They know what they have to do. You just hurry back home so you can tame this Kitty because she keeps purring for you," Yahnise said, getting wet just thinking about her husband waxing her ass.

"I will baby. Just take care of her until I can get there," EJ said laughing. "I love you," he said before hanging up.

* * * *

Later on that day, after they had deposited the money, they all went out sightseeing to have some fun. By the time they returned to their hotel room, they were tired as hell. EJ went to take a shower while the girls watched TV. After he took his shower, he put on basketball shorts and a wife beater. When he came out of the bathroom, Tiffany was eating and Denver was looking at all of the stuff she had purchased that day.

"Damn! Did you get enough shit while you were out shopping?" EJ said, looking at Denver.

"Boy please! You know a girl can never have enough clothes," she said, throwing a shirt at him. "I'm about to go and try on some of this stuff and take a hot shower," she said, heading for the bathroom.

EJ went over to the bed, sat down and started eating his food while him and Tiffany watched, "The Fast and The Furious." While EJ was watching the movie, he noticed that Denver never shut the bathroom door. He could see her standing in the bathroom with nothing on but a thong. She was trying on her clothes. He turned his head, but then he quickly turned back around and watched her for a few minutes. He thought she felt him watching her and purposely bent over giving him a full view of her pussy lips. His man instantly stood up. He got up, went over to the little refrigerator, and took out a soda. By the time he finished the soda and threw his empty food container in the trash, Denver was coming out of the bathroom.

She now had on a robe and some slippers. She picked up her under clothes and went back in the bathroom to take her shower.

"I'll be back in a few minutes. I'm going down to get something out of the car," EJ said as he headed for the door.

"Okay and bring my purse back up with you. I left it in the backseat," Tiffany said before he walked out of the door.

EJ went down and sat in the car for about an hour talking to his wife and playing with his son over the phone. When he hung up with them, he called Ed, Chan, Wan, and Shannon to make sure that they were all okay and handling their business. By the time he got back upstairs, Tiffany and Denver were in the bed already asleep. He quietly sat down on the bed, took his shoes off, and laid down. He fell asleep in about ten minutes.

The next couple of days were going to be crucial for them. From Canada, they were headed to Puerto Rico, and then they were headed to Saint Croix. That would be their last stop before they headed home. They were expected to arrive back home early Sunday morning. If everything went well, they would have deposited over $960,000.00 into all of the accounts. That would surely put them right where they needed to be.

* * * *

Bless and Erica had been hanging out together for the past four days. They were getting very close, very fast. Bless couldn't get enough of her and she couldn't get enough of him. They were already fucking like wild animals everywhere and every chance they could. His plan was going better than he would have ever thought. He just had to put the next phase into motion.

They were laying on Erica's couch, all cuddled up watching "Meet the Browns." "So when are you going to introduce me to your brother?" Bless asked, kissing Erica on her neck.

"Ummmm... As soon as his ass gets some time. He is always busy with my other brother EJ. The both of them are always going out of town a lot handling business," she said, rubbing on his dick.

"Well do they need any extra help with their business?" Bless asked, trying to get some information out of her.

"They might need another worker. They are into all types of shit and they could probably use some extra help. I will talk to him as soon as I see him," she said. "Now stop talking about my brothers and put this in your mouth," Erica said pulling out one of her titties.

She and EJ only fucked that one time so she still looked at him like a brother and he still looked at her like his little sister. Neither one of them wanted to take it there again.

* * * *

At the Federal building on 6th and Market Street, Agent Kaplin and Detective Harris were going through all of the wire taps from the week, and were coming up empty handed.

"Out of all of these fucking recordings, we don't have anything to go on," Agent Kaplin said, leaning back in his chair.

"We are going to lose our wiretapping authorities if we don't get something soon," Detective Harris said.

"I got a plan, but it has to stay between us. It's going to be illegal, but if it works we will have what we need to grab them," Agent Kaplin said.

"Ohhhh hell! What is it and I hope I won't lose my job over it because just like you, I have a family to take care of," Detective Harris said, looking at his partner.

Agent Kaplin sat up in his chair. "Well I was thinking that we should tap into his mom's phone and see what we can get on her. After we catch her doing something illegal, we can lock her ass up and then we can see what she will give us. We will never tell her about the tap being illegal. I think if we find something on her, she will talk," Agent Kaplin said.

"Well fuck it then. Let's do it. I have your back all the way partner," Detective Harris said, pounding fist with Agent Kaplin.

* * * *

It was the last night of their business trip so they were out partying at a club in Saint Croix. Everything had gone smoothly and by the time they would return to Philly, all of the checks should have cleared. EJ, Tiffany, and Denver were sitting at a table having great time. Denver and Tiffany were drunk. EJ never drank so he was their bodyguard for the night.

"I'm so fucked up that I can't even walk right now," Denver said, leaning over at the table.

"Shit, me too! I'm not drinking anymore after tonight," Tiffany said, agreeing with her friend.

EJ just laughed at them, thinking that they both were crazy. Then a Reggae song came on and Tiffany and Denver stood up and started moving their hips to the beat. Then they went out on the dance floor and started grinding on each other. Their dancing was so sexual that this guy walked over and grabbed Tiffany's hips from behind trying to grind on her. It didn't help that they both were only wearing two piece bikinis.

Tiffany pushed the guy off of her and kept on dancing with Denver. This dude was persistent so he tried again. This time when Tiffany tried to push him off of her, he wouldn't let go. She started to knock his hands off of her when he wrapped his arms tightly around her waist.

EJ walked up to the man and politely loosened his grip on Tiffany's waist. "What the fuck are you doing to her?" he asked, standing face to face with the man who seemed to be drunk.

"What's your problem?" the man questioned. "Is she with you?" he questioned while sizing EJ up.

"Yeah, both of them are with me so now step the fuck off," EJ said and then turned around to walk off the dance floor. Before he could take a few steps, the man struck him, knocking him to the floor.

EJ was back on his feet with the quickness of a cat. As soon as he got to his feet, he hit the man with a two piece followed by a roundhouse. Then he hit him with an upper cut that knocked him out cold.

The bouncers quickly rushed over and threw EJ, Tiffany, and Denver out of the club. The trio were mad as hell because some random drunk dude had ruined their night. Instead of going somewhere else, they decided to go back to their hotel room. When they got to their room, EJ went in the bathroom to take a shower so that he could hurry and get in the bed. He wanted to be up and fresh because they had an early morning flight.

While he was in the shower, he heard Reggae music in the room. "Y'all didn't get enough of that music before we got kicked out of the club?" he yelled to the girls, laughing.

As he was drying off and putting on his basketball shorts, he thought he heard something that sounded like a moan, but he paid it no mind.

When he walked into the room, he couldn't believe his eyes.

Denver and Tiffany were on the bed kissing each other while they both had their bikini bottoms pulled to the side fingering each other. Denver looked up and saw him watching. "Sit in that chair and enjoy the show. We are just releasing some much needed stress," she said, looking at EJ.

EJ went and sat down in the chair next to the bed as he was told to do. He looked at the women in amazement. They began tongue kissing again and at the sight of the sexual act, EJ's dick started to get hard.

After a couple of minutes, Tiffany slid her bikini bottom off and

Denver followed suit. Then Tiffany began to moan while she rubbed and massaged her own clit while Denver and EJ watched. Denver's pussy was getting extremely wet at just the sight of Tiffany playing with herself.

"Come eat my pussy," Tiffany seductively said to Denver. Denver complied as she leaned over and thrust her tongue inside Tiffany's warm wet pussy. She was licking and slurping on Tiffany's pussy so loud that EJ's erection was now brick hard. She was switching back and forth from tongue fucking Tiffany to sucking on her clit. Then she locked her lips on Tiffany's clit and slid two of her fingers in her pussy. Tiffany gasped for air through clenched teeth.

"Oh shit! Damn baby!" Tiffany said out of breath, as she grabbed Denver's head and begged her not to stop. Seconds later, Tiffany's body tensed up as she began to cum. Once she was finished sucking on Tiffany's pussy, Denver laid on her back and let Tiffany please her as well. After the two women finished eating each other out, they wanted a man in on the action.

EJ's dick was rock hard from the show and pre cum was seeping out of the head.

"Take off all of your clothes and come over here," Denver said. Without hesitation, EJ was out of his clothes and on the bed within a minute. Denver and Tiffany both started massaging his dick looking at each other to see who would deep throat it first.

Denver slowly began to lick around the rim of his dick with the tip of her tongue while Tiffany dipped her head beneath his balls and started sucking on them. Both of the girls took turns sucking and licking on his dick and balls until he came which didn't take very long.

When he came, the girls were play fighting over which one was going to swallow it.

After that, they still were not done with him. They continued to suck and lick on his dick until he was hard again. Once they got him hard again, they both took turns riding him. One of the girls would ride his face while the other one rode his dick. This was an all-out orgy. They were sucking and fucking each other into sexual bliss. This orgy lasted for a few hours. Neither of the three thought about their early flight in the morning. Hopefully they wouldn't be too tired and oversleep. They really couldn't afford to miss their flight.

CHAPTER 22

EJ and the girls had just returned from their trip yesterday. Since it was Monday, he decided to do some work at the house on 56th Street. He was turning on the block when he got a call from Ed's mom. "Hello," he said, parking his car.

"I need to talk to you when you get a minute," Ms. Cynthia said, as she cooked her breakfast.

"Okay well I'm in Southwest right now. I can stop over there in about an hour," EJ said, checking his watch for the time.

"That will be good. I have some things to do this morning and I should be back by then," she said, as she put her eggs on her bagel and took a bite.

"Call me when you are on your way back and I will leave out then, so that I can be there when you get there," EJ said, as he hung up.

He wanted to update everyone's accounts and move the money out of the banks that they had deposited the checks in on their trip. Those accounts were only to clear the checks. Once they cleared, they had a corporate account where they would wire the money. It was so easy to do it that way just in case one of the checks didn't clear, or if it put up a red flag for some reason, it wouldn't affect the other checks that did clear.

EJ became a pro at this thanks to Chan who had taught him everything. He knew all the ins and outs of the business.

What he wanted to do today was create some blank business checks, so all he would have to do is put a name on it when it was time to use it.

Two hours later EJ had made twenty checks. They were all for the same amount of $2,500.00. If he walked into a bank to cash them, he wouldn't have any problems because they were from an investment company. Then he made four without an amount on them just in case he had to put a different amount on them.

"As he was about to check his overseas account, his cell phone rang. "Hey Ms. Cynthia, I'm so sorry. I forgot all about you. Where are you now?" EJ said, typing on the keyboard.

"I'm at the McDonald's on 60th and Woodland Avenue," she said.

"I'll tell you what, swing pass the crib I'm at right now and we can talk here," EJ said.

"Okay, where are you at?" Ms. Cynthia asked pulling out of the McDonald's.

"I'm on 56th and Elmwood. When you get to the corner, call me and I will come outside," EJ said, while looking at his account.

"You might as well come out now because I'm almost at 57th and Elmwood. I will be there when the light changes," Ms. Cynthia said.

"I'm coming outside now," EJ said, hanging up the phone. He never ever brought anybody to this house outside of his partners, but he wanted to finish his work so he could spend the day with his son and Ms. Cynthia was Ed's mom, so she was cool.

He went outside and walked to the corner to meet Ms. Cynthia. Once he saw her, he told her where to park and they walked back to his house. He noticed something was different about Ed's mom. She looked like she was getting thinner than she already was. Her hair wasn't even done and that was not like Ms. Cynthia to go out of the house without her hair done.

"Is everything okay with you?" EJ asked as they sat on the couch in the living room.

"Well, not really. I really need to get some extra money from somewhere," she said, sounding concerned.

"Why? What's wrong?" EJ questioned. He knew that Ed gave his mom enough money every month to last her for a couple of months. Something wasn't right and he wanted to know what it was.

"What I say here stays between us. Can you promise me that?" Ms. Cynthia said, getting up and sitting in the chair facing EJ.

EJ looked at her puzzled. "I can't promise you that until I know what's going on," he said.

She looked at him for a moment before speaking. "Well about a month ago, I was holding Ed's drugs at my house and I got a little curious as to what white people see in this stuff. So anyway, I said to myself that if I tried it, I wouldn't get addicted to it. I tried it once and everything was cool. About a week later, I tried it again because I was thinking about it. After that, I started wanting it more and more until the next thing I knew, I was smoking it almost every day," she said as her legs started opening and closing.

EJ happened to be looking down because he was trying not to look in her eyes and he noticed that she wasn't wearing any panties under her skirt. He immediately got up and stood by her. She continued to talk.

"Well Ed don't keep that stuff around anymore since he got locked up so I had to start buying it from someone to support my habit. Now I owe him a whole lot of money and he said if I don't pay him that he will hurt me," she said, as tears ran down her face.

"Exactly how much do you owe this person," EJ asked sounding pissed.

"I owe him $5,000.00 because I borrowed a lot from him throwing all these get high parties," Ms. Cynthia said.

"What the fuck did you just say?" EJ asked sounding furious. "I got to tell Ed about this and then we are going to put you in rehab."

"No, don't tell my kids, please EJ. That's why I came to you," she said nervously.

"I can't let you do this. I have to tell him because he would do the same for me," EJ said pulling out his cell phone to call his friend.

Ms. Cynthia stood up, grabbed his phone, and put it behind her back. "Please EJ; I will do anything you ask. Just don't call him," she said, trying not to let him get his phone.

"I'm calling him no matter what so give me my damn phone," EJ said, getting mad.

She sat back on the couch hiding EJ's phone behind her under the pillow so he couldn't get it. "EJ please don't do this. I'll suck your dick and I'll let you fuck this sweet pussy," Ms. Cynthia said lifting up her skirt showing him her pussy.

EJ became enraged at this and quickly moved her out of the way and grabbed his phone.

"I'm calling Ed right now so you might as well stop begging," EJ said, as he dialed Ed's phone number.

Ms. Cynthia looked at him with hate in her eyes. "Fuck you then! I'll get you back for this," she said as she got up and started to leave. As she was walking towards the door, she noticed a few blank checks sitting on the table. She looked back to see what EJ was doing and then snatched a couple of the checks and rushed out the door.

EJ didn't even know that he had just made a big mistake by bringing her to this house. The damage had only just begun.

* * * *

Ed couldn't believe what EJ was telling him. "Where is she at right now?" he said even madder than EJ.

"I don't know. She ran out the house when I said I was calling you. I should have taken her car keys. Ed, I'm worried about her man. I called Ms. Sheila and she told me who they were getting the drugs from," EJ said.

"Who?" Ed asked, ready to kill the person who helped support his mom's habit.

"She said it was some dude named Ramee. He be around that way with your sister's boyfriend. I'm searching for the nigga ASAP and when I do find him, I'm gonna rock him to sleep," EJ said without saying another word.

"I'mma call Erica right now," Ed said, hanging up the phone.

As soon as Ed dialed Erica's number, it went straight to voicemail. He hung up and tried to call her again, but he got the same result so he decided to leave her a message this time. "Yo, hit me the fuck up as soon as you get this message! It's an emergency!"

"What's wrong baby?" Tamara asked, coming out of the bathroom butt naked from taking a shower after having sex with her man.

"My mom is out there tripping. I have to go to Philly right quick to see what's going on," Ed said, getting dressed.

"Do you want me to go with you?" Tamara asked.

"Yes I do. Come on baby, get dressed, and ride with me," he said, putting his shoes on.

* * * *

Ms. Cynthia had left EJ's spot mad as hell. "He think he can just say fuck me and get away with it. I'll show him. I raised his ass along with my kids. How dare he tell me no!" she said out loud, driving down Lindbergh Boulevard all crazy.

She started looking at the checks she had just stolen from EJ. Then a thought came to her mind. "I'm going to cash a couple of these and get the money I need plus some," she said smiling.

The bank name on the checks was Melon PSFS. She knew it was one on Island Avenue so she headed in that direction.

When she got there, she sat in the car for a few minutes thinking about how much she should make the out for checks. She decided to make one for $2,500.00 and if that worked, she would go to another bank and make the next check out for more.

Ms. Cynthia went in the bank, walked right up to a teller, and endorsed the check. Then she gave it to the teller. After a couple of minutes, the teller stood up and said, "I'll be right back in a minute ma'am."

After a couple of minutes, the manager walked out of the back and said, "Ms. Young could you please come with me?"

Ms. Cynthia got alarmed and started running toward the door. The guard at the door was already waiting for her and he grabbed her as she tried to pass him.

"Get off of me! Get your hands off of me!" she said screaming.

Within minutes, two police cars were pulling up and the officers hurriedly ran into the bank. They arrested Ms. Cynthia and took her away.

Two Hours Later

Agent Kaplin and Detective Harris were sitting at a desk in Central Booking. Agent Kaplin's phone started ringing. He took his cell out and answered, "Hello. Agent Kaplin speaking."

"Hi, this is Officer Bryant from over on 65th and Woodland. We just brought in a suspect for trying to cash a fraudulent check. You and Detective Harris' name comes up whenever something like this happens so I called you," the officer said.

"Is it a male or a female?" Agent Kaplin asked snapping his fingers at Detective Harris as he jumped up grabbing his jacket and heading to the door.

"It's a female and she looks like she was trying to get some get-high money. The name that is on her license is a Ms. Cynthia Young," Officer Bryant said waiting for an answer.

"Do not let her go and don't charge her! We are on our way there now!" Agent Kaplin said, hanging up.

He looked at Detective Harris and said, "We got her ass now baby boy. Let's go pay Ms. Young a visit."

* * * *

When they arrived at the station, they flashed their badges, and headed straight for the holding cells. When they got there and saw Ms. Cynthia, they couldn't believe how much she had changed since the last time they had saw her.

She looked thinner and her hair wasn't done. She still had that beautiful young face though.

"Ms. Young grab your stuff and come with us," Detective Harris said pulling out a pair of cuffs.

When she looked up and saw them standing there, she became instantly nervous. She stood up and walked to the door where Detective Harris put the cuffs on her. The turn key opened the door and she was led out of the holding area.

Detective Harris took her out to the police car while Agent Harris grabbed the evidence from the property clerk. "You're in some real trouble now, but what I want to know is what happened to you?" Detective Harris said, looking in the backseat of the unmarked Crown Victoria. He noticed that her legs were open and that she didn't have on any panties.

A devious grin came across his face, as he wanted to see how far he could go with her. He could tell by her appearance that she was now using drugs so he thought he would have a little fun while Agent Kaplin was still in the building.

"What if I can get you out of this situation?" Detective Harris asked, turning in his seat so that he could watch her.

She looked up at him as his eyes stayed glued to her pussy. "What do I have to do?" she asked.

"First I want you to lift your skirt up some more so that I can see that wet pussy of yours," he said.

She looked at his suspiciously at first, but then she thought about it, and said, "Will you let me go if I do?" Ms. Cynthia just wanted to get out of here and go home. She wasn't thinking about anything else.

"You won't go home yet, but it will make things a lot easier for you to go if you work with me," he said, waiting to see what she was going to do.

She opened her legs exposing her vagina so that Detective Harris could see.

"Now I want you to play with yourself and make it real wet until you come," he said getting aroused. He reached in the back, uncuffed her hands from behind her back, and cuffed them in front of her.

She started massaging her pussy until she started moaning and biting down on her bottom lip. She was really getting into it until she came all over her finger. "Is that all you wanted to see?" she asked, breathing hard.

"Yes, that's it for now. We will talk more when we get to the Federal Building. I might want to see you again," he said as Agent Kaplin walked out the building towards the car. "Don't say anything about what just happened and you will be okay," Detective Harris said turning around as Ms. Cynthia fixed her skirt.

Agent Kaplin got in the car and said, "We have the missing piece to this puzzle." He looked at Detective Harris and held up the checks that were found in Ms. Cynthia's purse and the one she had tried to cash.

"Now all we have to do is get the person who is making them," he said as he started the car and pulled off.

Ms. Cynthia was sitting in the backseat listening and she started thinking about the argument she had just had earlier with EJ. A smile came across her face as she leaned back in the seat and waited to get to the Federal Building. What she really wanted was some dope and she would do whatever she had to do to get some even if it meant giving up some pussy.

CHAPTER 23

Erica and Bless had just finished having sex and she wanted to take a shower. "I'm about to take a shower before we go to the mall," she said, heading for the bathroom.

Just before she went in, she heard her phone beep. She walked over to the dresser and picked up her phone. She seen that she had some missed calls from her brother. "Damn, my brother called me a few times. I better call him back right quick," she said.

"See if he can do something for me now since you are about to call him," Bless said as he laid back on the bed.

"Okay baby, I'll ask when I talk to him," Erica said calling her brother. After a couple of rings, she got his voicemail.

Then Erica's phone went off again and it was Ed. "Hey what's up Ed?" Erica said, turning the water on in the shower.

"Yo, who is this nigga that you have been fucking with?" Ed asked angry.

"Why? What's going on Ed and why are you yelling at me like that?" Erica asked getting angry.

"That motherfucker been selling dope to mommy and when I get my hands on that clown I'mma rip his fucking heart out. Where the fuck is he?" Ed said.

Erica was trying to process everything her brother was saying. She could not believe what he had just said. "Mommy is on what?"

"She's on that shit thanks to your clown ass boyfriend. She owes him five stacks from him loaning her that shit for some get-high parties. Now tell me where he is so I can come see him," he said sounding irritated.

"He is here. Where are you at?" she said.

Ed was in Delaware trying to get information on the clown from one of the niggas that knew him. "I'll be there in less than an hour. You just keep him there," he said and hung up the phone.

Erica couldn't even take a shower now. She had to make sure her mom was okay. She called her mom and her phone went straight to voicemail. She hung up and tried five more times only to get the same result.

She was about to go in the room when she heard Bless on his phone with somebody. "I have her ready to introduce me to that nigga now. As soon as he comes here, I'm gonna murk him and her," she heard him say.

Erica was about to have a panic attack. *"Who the fuck is this nigga,"* she was thinking to herself. *"Now he don't know who the fuck he is dealing with,"* she thought to herself before walking into another room.

She texted her brother to meet her at the Karmen Suite Apartments on Island Avenue. That's where Bless was staying. She gave him the address and he texted her right back, "be careful sis!"

Erica put on some tights and went back into the room where Bless was. "Come on we are going to your house and wait for my brother. He is going to meet us there with the work," she said, putting a wife beater on.

"That's what's up. Let's go," he said, putting on his shoes.

Ten minutes later, they were at his crib. Erica was trying to think of something to make her relax until Ed got there. "Take your clothes off and let me give you some head before he gets here," she said knowing that would work.

"Now that's what I'm talking about. You sure know how to treat your man. Bring that ass over here and put those juicy lips on this dick," he said, taking off his pants.

Erica sat her purse down next to her as she got on her knees and began giving him a blow job.

"Oh shit baby! Do that shit!" he said as he closed his eyes and enjoyed what Erica was doing to him.

She was sucking his dick and watching him at the same time. When he closed his eyes to enjoy the blow job, she quickly put her free hand on something in her purse. As soon as he was about to cum, Erica took the bag ass pair of scissors out of her purse and put them to his dick.

"Don't fucking move or I will cut your dick off," Erica said slowly.

Bless jumped, but he couldn't move. He was scared straight. "What are you doing baby?"

"Don't fucking baby me, nigga! So you are selling my mom drugs and you want to kill me and my brother, huh?" she said still holding the scissors to his dick.

"Come on Erica! I really don't know what you are talking about!" Bless said sounding a little nervous.

"Nigga, I heard you on the phone and don't worry because my brothers have something for you when they get here," she said.

Bless knew he wasn't going to get out of here alive so he tried something else. "I love you Erica. Please don't do this to me. Ramee did that to your mom. Please just let me go and I will set him up for you."

At first Bless thought, he was getting somewhere until he felt a sharp pain near his dick. When he looked down, she was standing up holding his dick in her hand. Blood was gushing out of the area where his penis used to be. The pain was so unbearable that he damn near went into shock.

Erica took his severed dick and shoved it in his mouth. Then she quickly went in her purse and pulled out her 32 that Ed had gave her for protection. She pointed at his head and squeezed the trigger.

POP! POP! POP! POP! POP! POP! POP! CLICK! CLICK! CLICK!

Erica kept squeezing as she unloaded every shot into his head. She seemed possessed until her cell phone started ringing bringing her back to reality.

She looked down at the screen and saw that it was Ed calling her. She went to the door and let him in.

As soon as she opened the door, Ed and EJ were standing there, with guns in their hand. They saw blood on her clothes and hands. She was still holding the smoking gun also.

"Where's that nigga at Erica?" EJ said as he burst in the door looking for Bless.

She looked up at her brother and started crying. Ed grabbed her and put his arms around her. "It's okay sis. We are here now," he said, holding his little sister tight.

EJ came back to the door with Erica's purse. "Come on! We have to get the fuck out of here now! The cops might be here any minute now!" he said as they ran to the car, jumped in, and took off.

The crime scene that they had just left would be on every news channel for the next month. It was the most gruesome scene that anyone had seen in years. Their work wasn't done though. That still had to find Ramee and kill him as well and they had to do it fast before he found out about his boy.

* * * *

When EJ gabbed Erica's purse, he also grabbed Bless' cell phone. They went straight to Ed's mom house to wait for her to come home when a text came across Bless cell phone. EJ looked at it and read the message out loud.

"Did you kill the bitch and her brother yet?"

EJ immediately texted back.

"Mission Accomplished. Meet me at 29th and Huntington at 8:00 p.m. I will be there with the work and money I took."

To his surprise, Ramee texted right back asking for the address. EJ said to himself, "This nigga is dumb as shit!" He gave him the address to one of Ed's old trap houses and then he explained to Ed what had happened.

"Yo Ed," EJ said looking in Erica's room for him. He wasn't in there so he went downstairs and saw Ed cursing at someone on the phone. When he hung up, EJ asked, "Who was that?"

Ed looked up at his friend and said, "I'm officially out of the game. That was Twan on the phone. I told him that after all of this is gone, I'm gone."

EJ looked at Ed and wondered why the all of a sudden change of heart. "Are you sure man?"

"Yeah dawg, after hearing that shit about my mom, I decided to stop. After all, it was my shit that got her hooked in the first place," Ed said.

"Well strap up because it's time for payback. That nigga Ramee is going to meet us at the trap house on Huntington Street at eight. It's time to put him on ice for good," EJ said cocking his 9mm back.

"Let's do it," Ed said as he grabbed his vest off of the floor and put it on.

They headed out the door so that they could get to the spot before Ramee got there. They had something special for that nigga.

* * * *

When they arrived at the trap house, Ed popped the trunk and grabbed the AK-47 and the AR-15 out of the trunk.

"What do we need all that for? It's only going to be him coming to meet his partner. Remember, your dead," EJ said smiling

Ed shut the trunk and passed the AR-15 to EJ. "You can never be too sure of someone like him. He might think it's a setup," he said, walking in the door with EJ right on his heels.

They were looking out the window when Ramee's black Grand Marquis pulled up and parked. Ramee stepped out of the car and headed for the house. He was by himself until another car pulled up. Ramee turned around and waited as the person turned their engine off and stepped out of their Mercedes Benz.

Ed and EJ couldn't believe their luck when they saw YG walking towards Ramee. "I guess we are going to kill two birds with one stone," Ed said, cocking the AK-47.

YG and Ramee walked in the building and started looking around. "Where in the hell is this nigga at?" YG asked.

"We're right here pussy boy," Ed said pointing the AK at them while EJ came up on them from the other side aiming the AR-15 in their direction.

They both thought they had saw a ghost as their eyes lit up. "Wha... Wha... What the hell is this about? Where is Bless?" Ramee stuttered.

Ed said laughing. "He met the devil a few hours ago and so will the both of you soon. I'm going to have some fun watching you die slow, you bitch ass nigga," Ed said as he put the AR-15 down and grabbed the rope he had on the floor.

"Get on your hands and knees nigga," EJ said to Ramee, waiting to tie him up.

"Fuck you! I ain't doing shit!" Ramee said, with a lot of confidence because he didn't want to go out like a bitch.

"Oh yeahhhhh?" EJ said pulling out his 9mm from behind his back.

BLOC! BLOC!

Ramee felt both shots hit his knee caps. He screamed out in pain as he fell to the floor.

BLOC! BLOC! BLOC! BLOC! BLOC! BLOC!

EJ let off six more shots as he hit Ramee in his chest and stomach.

He then walked up to him, pointed his gun at his head, and put two more bullets right between his eyes.

BLOC! BLOC!

"That's for my Step-Mom, you pussy!" he said looking at the dead corpse laying in a pool of blood.

Ed and YG both looked at EJ. They both grew nervous when they looked in his eyes. Ed didn't recognize his own friend and YG was scared because he didn't know what was about to happen to him.

"Tie this bitch ass nigga up and let's have some fun," EJ said to his friend.

Ed tied YG to the bed frame on his stomach. He spread his legs apart and duct taped his mouth.

"So you want to see what it feels like to be disrespected nigga?" Ed asked as he took a knife and cut YG's suit pants off. He then took the broom and stuck it up in YG's ass.

YG screamed out in excruciating pain, but the sound was muted from the duct tape over his mouth. EJ then came over and poured acid from the car battery over his feet and legs. That sent him into shock.

"Hell no, we're not done yet," Ed said as he grabbed his AK and pulled the broom stick out of his ass replacing it with the AK. "I'll see you in hell nigga, but for now enjoy yourself," he said as he pulled the trigger to the AK and watched as a bullet went through his ass and out of his head.

Ed didn't stop firing until the AK was empty. He looked at EJ with the same look that he saw in his eyes a few minutes ago. It was at that very moment that they both knew that if anyone ever harmed either one of them or their families, that they would be as good as dead because they would hunt them down and kill them.

EJ and Ed left the building without glancing back at the carnage that they had left behind. Tomorrow it would be business as usual, but tonight they were going to go home and chill with their families.

CHAPTER 24

January 20, 2013

Agent Kaplin sat in his office going over some paperwork that he had been ignoring since being on his current case. He didn't realize that the case he was looking at was linked to the fraud case. Someone was cashing in on fake tax returns. Last year alone, over $900,000.00 was claimed from fake W2s. He had been working with the IRS to get to the bottom of this.

Since it was income tax season again, they were working together to find out who was behind it all. Agent Kaplin's confidential informant (CI) was going to help him build a case. His informant was reliable and he had a good position inside the organization. He knew it wouldn't be long before the culprits would be brought to justice.

Just as he was finishing, he received a phone call. "Hello, Agent Kaplin speaking. How may I help you?" he said.

The caller didn't say anything immediately, but he finally spoke. "This is CI 201267 and I have information for you," the caller said.

"Go ahead and fill me in," Agent Kaplin said, writing the CI's security number down as he waited for the information.

"Well, they will be going into Beneficial Bank today to cash four checks. It will be three females and one male. The checks are from State Farm Insurance Company and they are all over $40,000.00. As soon as you get a minute, I need you to check your text messages. I sent all of their names to you," the caller said before hanging up.

Agent Kaplin checked his text message and wrote the names down on a piece of paper. He called Detective Harris as he ran out the door telling him to meet him at Beneficial Bank on 64th and Woodland Avenue in Southwest Philly.

He also called the bank to inform them of the possible check fraud that was going to take place today. He called his Commander and asked him to keep backup on standby just in case he needed them. This was the much needed break in the case and it finally came through.

The informant had been giving him information for the last couple of months. He had caught six people so far, but none of them gave up anything. They were only petty cases though. The most they were trying to cash was $2,000.00. That would only put them behind bars for maybe three months. It was nothing like this one though. If he caught the people from check cashing at Beneficial Bank he knew they would get a lengthy sentence if they didn't cooperate. Agent Kaplin started smiling as he headed to the back to meet Detective Harris.

* * * *

Ever since they took care of YG and his crew, business was back to normal. Ed hadn't touched any drugs since giving Tuck his operation. He and EJ were just about to leave Foot Locker when EJ said, "I think it's time to get our accounts to the point where they need to be. We have everything we want at the touch of a button. So let's try to make our quota within the next few months."

Ed didn't know what EJ was talking about at first, but then it all came to him. "So how do you want to do that? You are the brains of this operation," Ed said, as they walked to the car.

"Well we can start selling people credit cards," EJ said as he placed the bag in the trunk.

Ed looked at his friend wondering what the hell he was saying. "How do you expect us to do that?" he said as they got in the car.

"I talked to Chan and he can get us some corporate numbers that we can use. So what we want to do is if someone wants a credit line for say $5,000.00, we charge them half. Then we can make them a credit card using their name, but the company information of our choice. I checked Craigslist all morning trying to find a machine where to do this. They have one out in California that I ordered and it should be here in a couple of weeks," EJ said as they headed for Jersey on their way to Ed's crib.

"Wow! It sounds like you have everything all figured out, but where are we going to get cards from," Ed said.

"That's the easy part. They are the same card stock that the banks use to make debit cards. We have Ronald on the inside who can get us the merchandise that we need. So once we are ready to go, we'll have everything on lock. Checks, income taxes, license, and now credit cards will all be at our disposal," EJ said with a smile on his face.

Ed was just as excited because he knew that they were about to make a whole lot of money. With that being said, EJ turned on Meek Millz, I'm a Boss, and the two bobbed their heads as they headed over the bridge.

* * * *

In the meanwhile, over at the Beneficial Bank on 64th and Woodland, Agent Kaplin and Detective Harris had just arrived. They exited their car and went inside the bank. Agent Kaplin flashed his badge to the security guard and asked to speak to the Branch Manager. "I'm Agent Kaplin and this is my partner Detective Harris. We talked to you on the phone about a couple of fraudulent checks that may be cashed here today," Agent Kaplin said, sitting in the Branch Manager's office.

"Yes and so far none of the names that we spoke about came through here yet," the manager said.

"Well if you don't mind, we would like to hang out for a while and see if anything happens," Detective Harris said.

"No, not at all gentleman. Make yourselves comfortable. Do you want any coffee or maybe a soda?" the manager asked.

"Some coffee will be just fine," Agent Kaplin said picking up a magazine.

About forty-five minutes had passed before a couple of college kids walked into the bank. To everyone else the seemed like normal customers coming to get money from the account their parents had probably set up for them, but to Agent Kaplin, they fit the description of the people they were waiting for.

"You see those four kids right there, John? They just might be the people we are looking for," Agent Kaplin said pointing to the kids signing something at the table.

"Yeah, let's just wait it out and see what they do. We don't want to blow the chance to hit a big one," Detective Harris aid watching their every move.

Lyric had said that she would cash her check first to make sure everything was okay. She was a friend of Jamie's, she had been cashing checks for about six months now, and she had made plenty of money. She always preferred to go first so that if nobody else got a chance to cash their check, well at least she had cashed hers. If she would have been aware of her surroundings, she might have let someone else go first today, or better yet, she would have left right back out of the bank as quickly as she entered.

Lyric went up to the teller and handed her the check and her ID. "Good morning, I'm just here to cash my insurance checks," she said to the teller.

"Do you have an account with us because in order to cash a check for this amount, you have to at least have an account here," the teller said.

"Yes I do have an account and my account number is 1110436542," Lyric said as the teller punched the numbers into her computer.

"Yes, here we are. Ms. Smith would you like it all now or do you want to deposit some?" the teller asked.

"I'll take it all now," she said excitedly.

The teller began counting the money and at the same time, she gave her manager a head nod letting him know this was one of the checks that they were expecting.

The manager signaled the two officers and they walked out of the manager's booth office and over to Lyric.

As soon as the other kids saw the officers approaching, one of them yelled, "Lyric, let's go now," but it was too late for her to do anything. The other kids ran out of the door with Detective Harris in pursuit.

"Don't move! I'm a Federal Agent and you are under arrest!" Agent Kaplin said, showing his badge.

Lyric just stood there scared as she put her hands behind her back and Agent Kaplin put the cuffs on her. She had only been locked up one time before and that was for stealing a pair of earrings out of the Gallery on 9th and Market Street downtown. This was a little bit more serious so she didn't know what to do.

Agent Kaplin read her, her rights as he escorted her to the police car that was outside waiting.

Detective Harris had managed to catch one of the other girls that tried to get away. The other cops were searching for the other two.

"Well we got two out of four. I'm quite sure that we'll get the other two," Detective Harris said, putting the other girl in the police car.

"Yeah, they can't get that far that fast. Our backup was here in no time. I wish it had been agents instead of uniforms. Then we would have had them inside the bank instead of waiting for them blocks away," Agent Kaplin said.

"Well it ain't no reason to complain over spilled milk. Let's get these two down to the station and see what we can get out of them," Detective Harris said as he and Agent Kaplin got in their car to leave.

They were going to get something out of these two girls today and they were not going to quit until they did. What they really didn't know was that the information that they would get would lead them on a wild goose chase, but in the end, it would amazingly get them to the bottom of everything. Once they got to the bottom, it would be just a matter of time until they worked their way back to the top.

* * * *

Ms. Cynthia was sitting in the house watching the news when she heard someone knocking at her door. She went to answer it and when she looked through the peephole, she saw that it was Cathy from down the street. She opened the door and let her friend in. "Hey girl, what' took you so long to answer the damn door," Cathy said as she took her coat off trying to get some heat.

"I was watching the news. What's up with you? Did the gas go off at your house again?" Cynthia asked. The only time Cathy would come over at this hour of the night was when her gas was off or she wanted a fix.

"Yeah it's off and plus I have something for us to snack on," Cathy said as she pulled out a package from her pocket.

Ms. Cynthia's eyes lit up with anticipation as she stared at the package in Cathy's hand. Ever since she had confided in EJ and he had told Ed, she had been keeping it a secret that she still got high. Everyone thought that she had kicked her habit, but in all actuality, she had just became a pro at hiding it.

The only time she used was when no one was around and when she was with Cathy. She was even able to keep her job at the Parking Authority. No one suspected her to be doing anything like using drugs. She even started keeping her weight up by eating a lot during the day and right before she went to bed.

Ed and EJ gave her a job. They had put her in charge of keeping track of the workers to give her something to do when she wasn't at work. All she really had to do was tell the workers what banks to go to when EJ or

Ed called her. In return, Ed made sure that her bills were never late and he bought her a new Chrysler 300 because she said her other car had gotten stolen. What had really happened to her car was she had loaned it to some drug dealers so they could go to the club one night when she needed a fix. They never brought her car back and two weeks later the police found it stripped in a parking lot off of Orkney Street in North Philly.

"Let's go in the kitchen. Erica won't be home tonight so we have the house all to ourselves," Ms. Cynthia said, heading to the kitchen with Cathy behind her.

"So is it okay if I stay her with you tonight then?" Cathy asked, sitting at the table.

"Girl have I ever let you stay in that cold ass house whenever you gas was cut off before? As a matter of fact, let's just go to my room just in case someone pops up unexpectedly," Ms. Cynthia said, heading to her bedroom.

When they got in the room, they sat on the bed and Cathy pulled out her kit bag that she always carried around containing all types of paraphernalia. She had lighters, rubber strips to tie around your arm, glass dicks (pipes), etc. She always came prepared to get high.

She passed the bag to Ms. Cynthia and when she looked at it, she noticed that it was different. "What is this that we are about to use?" she asked looking at her friend.

Cathy grabbed the bag back from her and said, "This is something better than what we had before. It's heroin."

Ms. Cynthia was dumbfounded for a few seconds. "What? Girl I have never done that before and I don't think I want to try it now," she said.

"This is simple and you will love it," Cathy said, pulling the needle out of her bag.

Ms. Cynthia thought about it for a couple of minutes and then she said, "Fuck it! I can stop whenever I want, just like with crack."

Cathy laughed and said, "Girl you are crazy. Let me do you first so that way you will get the full feeling of it. Watch how it takes you to a whole new world."

Ms. Cynthia sat on the bed and Cathy pulled a chair up and sat in front of her. She then wrapped the rubber tie around her arm and tapped it to make her veins popped. Once she saw her veins appear, she melted the heroin, filled the needle up, and asked Ms. Cynthia if she was ready.

"Yeah, I'm ready. I'm no bitch. Bring it on," she said, even though she was a little nervous.

Cathy stuck the needle in and inserted the liquid substance into Ms. Cynthia's arm. Ms. Cynthia leaned back on the bed in total bliss. It felt so good to her that she had this tingling sensation in her shorts. What she didn't know is that it had gave her an orgasm.

Cathy then did the same thing to herself and the same feeling came across her. She leaned back in the chair and enjoyed the feeling.

After about ten minutes, they both felt hot. They didn't know if it was from the heat or the fact that they were high as hell off of the heroin.

Cathy began taking her pants and shirt off. Then she sat back down just feeling good in her panties and bra.

"I thought I was the only one burning up like that," Ms. Cynthia said as she took off her shorts that she was wearing with no panties. She then took of her shirt exposing her nice size titties. She wasn't wearing a bra either. Cathy knew how beautiful Ms. Cynthia was, but she didn't expect her body to be so perfect. She wasn't into girls, but she couldn't help but to get wet at the sight of Ms. Cynthia's slightly furry pussy.

Ms. Cynthia laid back down on the bed. "I'm really feeling good right now, Cathy. You should have been told me about this stuff," she said as she put her legs up showing her pussy hole.

Cathy sat in the chair and stared at Ms. Cynthia's pussy. She began feeling horny and wondered what it would taste like. Curiosity got the best of her as she slid between Ms. Cynthia's legs and stuck her tongue out and licked her clit.

Ms. Cynthia was so high that she didn't even jump. She just laid there with her eyes closed.

Cathy took that as an invitation to keep going. She stared off slow and sensual and then she sped up her pace as she started eating Ms. Cynthia's pussy like there was no tomorrow.

Ms. Cynthia started moaning and groaning while grabbing Cathy's head. She started pumping her pussy into Cathy's tongue as if it was a dick. "Yes baby, eat my pussy. Your tongue feels so good. Fuck me with your fingers, baby," Ms. Cynthia said as she spread her legs open even wider.

Cathy stuck one, two, three fingers into Ms. Cynthia's pussy and she came within in minutes. Then Cathy stood up and took her panties and bra off. Ms. Cynthia got the clue, got up, and pushed Cathy down on the bed. She sucked and licked on Cathy's pussy so good that she came within minutes. Then Ms. Cynthia got on top of Cathy in the 69 position the two women licked each other pussies as a cat licks his paw. They were so tired from having so many orgasms that they fell asleep with their pussies intertwined together. For Ms. Cynthia, this was the beginning of the trouble still to come. After this one episode, her life would never be the same.

CHAPTER 25

Chan and EJ were sitting in the car in front of Chan's house talking about what had happened yesterday.

"How the hell did they know that they would be at that bank? We don't even use that bank that often," Chan said to his partner.

"I'm not sure man. That shit is crazy. I can see if it was one of the other banks, which we use all of the time, but it wasn't. That brings the total up to eight. It could have easily been ten if the other two hadn't got away," EJ said frustrated.

"Yeah, I hired a lawyer to go down there and try to get them out on bail or something. If possible, he should be getting them out as soon as he can," Chan said.

"Just make sure that they don't link it back to us. We have too much going on right now and we can't afford to get caught up," EJ said, sipping his hot chocolate.

"I fell you bro. As soon as they come home, I'll meet up with them and see exactly what they have on them," Chan said.

"Now on to some other shit. Did you get the equipment that we need yet for the credit card numbers," EJ asked.

"Yeah, this is it right here, but this one doesn't belong to us," Chan said, pulling out a device that was so small you would hardly even know it was there. "All we have to do is put it on any credit card reader and whenever someone swipes their card, it will store their information in it. Then all we have to do is load it onto our computer and print up a card in someone else name," Chan said.

"I'll be glad when our stuff gets here. That is the last piece to our success. Once we get that, we will be able to do everything we need to do to reach our goal. Give them a call tomorrow and see if they can expedite our stuff in three days. Whatever it cost, just take it out of the petty cash account. If they want more money for that, then give it to them. Money is not an issue. Remember you have to spend it to make it," EJ said.

"I'm on it. You be safe and go home and get you some rest because you look tired," Chan said messing with EJ.

EJ really was tired though. He had been putting in a lot of time and work trying new things to make money. Even when he was home with his family, he would be on his laptop. Yahnise cursed him out about it quite a few times. That's why he had planned a vacation the weekend of Valentine's Day. They were going to Saint Thomas. It was going to be EJ, Yahnise, Ziaire, Ed, and Tamara. EJ was even going to bring Yahnise's sister Mira along so she could watch Ziaire some of the time. He had it all planned and hopefully nothing would go wrong.

* * * *

Ed was on his way back from Bala Cynwyd. He had to pick up some packages for Chan from one Bala Plaza. He decided to stop at McDonald's on Cityline Avenue to get something to eat. When he walked in and went to the counter to order, he saw this beautiful white girl taking orders and he knew he had to have her.

After he placed his order, he asked her what time she get off of work. At first she didn't want to answer him, but it was something about the way that he smiled at her and that missing tooth that made her say, "I get off at four; why?"

"Because I'm coming back to take you home. Do you have a ride?" he asked, taking his food.

"No," the girl said as she smiled at him.

"Okay, I'll be parked out front whenever you're ready," Ed said as he left out of the store. "I'll be fucking her by tonight," he said to himself as he pulled out of the parking lot.

While he was driving down Belmont Avenue, he noticed that a Ford Taurus was following him. He didn't pay any attention to it at first, until he noticed that it was a black guy and a white guy in the car. The first thing he said to himself was, *"Cops!"*

He really wasn't worried about them because he was clean for sure this time. He just kept driving hoping that they would just leave him alone. When he got to Parkside Avenue, he made a right turn and then pulled over. He wanted to see what they wanted because he wasn't running from them. To his surprise, they kept going straight pass him so he pulled off and headed home.

* * * *

Agent Kaplin and Detective Harris knew they had been made so they kept going down Belmont Avenue. They knew where to find him if they needed to speak with him. "Do you think he got the message," Detective Harris said.

"Loud and clear. He knows now that if he does anything stupid that we will be on his ass," Agent Kaplin said.

They wanted to catch him doing something, but instead they got made. They headed back downtown to look at the photos that were taken at PNC. Agent Kaplin was hoping that he would be able to find someone in the photos in their database. Once he got a hit, it wouldn't be hard to catch them.

They were alerted about another bank being hit yesterday by their CI. When the man tried to leave, security snatched him up and arrested him.

By the time Agent Kaplin and Detective Harris arrived, he was already on his way to the station. They interrogated him for hours with no luck. He was booked and sent to CFCF until his preliminary hearing. That was their ninth arrest and they still didn't have anything. Detective Harris said to Agent Kaplin, "I'm going to have to pay a visit to my CI and find out why we keep running into dead ends. Even though we took nine people off the streets, we still don't have the one who is making them and I want that person!"

"Well, I will drop you off at your car and then I'll go look at the photos at the office. After that, I'm going home and make love to my wife. I've been neglecting her for a while now so it's time to spend some quality time with her. Our kids are away so it's time to play," Agent Kaplin said.

"I feel you on that. I might just do the same thing myself," Detective Harris said, giving his partner some dap. They drove the rest of the way in silence, just thinking about their wives.

* * * *

Over in West Philly, Denver and Shannon were at Sneaker Villa on 52nd Street buying some sneakers. They were getting their little cousins something for their birthdays. They had to get the same color in everything they purchased because their cousins were twins and they always dressed alike.

After they left Sneaker Villa, Denver wanted to go across the street to check her account at Citizen's Bank. "Shannon, walk with me across the street to the bank for a minute. I have to check my account balance," she said to her sister.

"Let's go. I can check mine too while we are at it," Shannon said.

When they walked in the bank, they both signed their names on the clipboard and waited for the customer service representative to call their names.

"Ms. Clark," the representative said signaling for one of them to come to his desk. "How can I help you today," he said, sitting at his desk.

"We both would like to check our balances," Shannon said as she took out her ID and passed it to the representative. Denver did the same thing since they both had accounts there.

"Okay, let me pull that up for you right now," the representative said, hitting some keys on his keyboard. After several minutes, the representative said, "Hmmmm, it seems we have a problem here. Hold on while I pull up the other account."

After a couple of minutes he said, "Ms. Clark and Ms. Clark it seems that both of your accounts have been frozen for some reason." The representative continued to type on his keyboard for a few seconds. "A check was kicked back (bounced) on the same day as another one was being deposited. The new one canceled out the other one, but then that bounced too," he said looking at the two beautiful ladies.

"How can that be? My money always clears," Denver said in shock.

"Wait here while I go and talk to the manager so I can see what we can do about this," the representative said.

As the representative got up and went to the manager's office, Denver looked at her sister and said, "I think we better get the fuck out of here before we end up in jail."

Shannon nodded at her sister and they both made their way to the door. Shannon went out the door first and the green light came on without a problem. Then Denver tried to leave and the light turned red. When she turned around, the manager, the bank representative, and the guard were heading her way. Denver turned back to her sister and whispered, "Go!"

Shannon didn't want to leave her sister, but it made no sense for her to stay. It was nothing she could do so she ran up the street towards Chestnut where they had parked. Once she got to the car and jumped in, she called the only person that she knew could help her sister.

* * * *

EJ and Ziaire were outside in the yard playing with his basketball. Little Ziaire was walking now and EJ said he was going to be a NBA star. "Come on Zi, catch the ball," EJ said as he rolled the ball to his son.

Yahnise was in the kitchen laughing at the boys outside playing, while she was doing the dishes. She had just started the dishwater when she heard EJ's phone going off. She picked it up off the table and looked at the screen.

When she saw Shannon's number, she answered it. "Hey girl, what's up with you?" she said, walking towards the glass sliding door leading to the yard.

"Is EJ around, Yahnise? My sister was just arrested at the bank that we use for our accounts," Shannon said crying.

"What?! Hold on while I get EJ," Yahnise said walking outside. "Baby, Shannon is on the phone. Come quick! It's an emergency!" she said handing him the phone.

EJ grabbed the phone from his wife and walked inside the house while she got Ziaire. "What's wrong Shannon?" he asked.

"Denver just got locked up at Citizen's Bank. We went to check out account balance and they said our accounts were frozen. Then we tried to leave, but Denver got stuck trying to get out of the door," she said.

"What bank were y'all at again?" EJ asked sitting down at the table.

"Citizen's on 52nd and Chestnut."

EJ was trying to think of which police station they would have taken her. Then it hit him. "They will be taking her to 55th and Pine. I'm going to call Savino now and get him over there ASAP. You go to the house and just wait for me to get there," EJ said as he grabbed his car keys.

"Which house EJ? They have my ID so they know where I live and they might get me next," she said sounding scared.

"Go to the meeting house. You know where the spare key is. I'll swing by there as soon as I stop at the precinct," EJ said hanging up.

He gave his wife and son a kiss and left out the door heading to Philly. He was wondering what the hell went wrong. Were all the checks going to start bouncing? His mind was going one hundred miles per hour trying to figure out his next move. Things were getting crazy now and he still didn't know who was giving up the information. He kept his circle tight so he knew that it wasn't anybody out of his circle. He couldn't think about that right now. He had to hurry up and find out what was going on with Denver. He called his lawyer and then put the pedal to the metal as he hauled ass to Philly.

* * * *

Agent Kaplin was finishing up on running the names that popped up on the screen. He had four more suspects that he was going after in the next couple of days. His wiretaps were starting to pay off now thanks to his CI. His informant had plenty of conversations with someone name EJ, Ed, Chan, and Wan.

All he needed now was a face to go with the names. He already knew Ed, but he had no clue as to who the rest of these people were.

Just as he was heading out of his office, the phone rang. "Yes, Agent Kaplin here." He listened for a few minutes and then said, "I'll be right there. Thanks for the call." He hung up the phone and ran out the door happy as hell. He wanted to see whom they had locked up now.

* * * *

Denver sat in the cold cell with five other girls. They all had been picked up for fighting at Bartrum High School. She sat by herself at the other end of the cell thinking about how long it would be before someone got her out of here.

One of the girls came over and sat next to her. "My name is Kimmy. What's yours?" she asked.

Denver looked at her, but didn't say a word. Then Kimmy said,

"That's Refeaha, Valarie, Beverly, and Ashley."

"I don't care what their names are and I sure don't give a fuck about what your name is either. Now can you please get the fuck away from me so that I can think about how I'm going to get out of here," she said to Kimmy.

"Anyway, I like those shoes you have on and I wanted to know are you going to give them to me or do I have to take them?" Kimmy said with a blank expression on her face.

Denver looked at her as if she was crazy. "What part of get the fuck out of here don't you understand? You cannot have my shoes and you or your little rug rats aren't taking anything from me," Denver said ready for whatever.

Kimmy's friends stood up ready to fight. Kimmy said to Denver, "Have it your way," as she tried to sneak her but Denver was ready for it.

Denver ducked the blow and countered with a hook. It landed right in the middle of Kimmy's face knocking her off of the bench. The other girls moved in for the kill. Denver tried to fight them off, but it was too many of them against her.

One of the officers heard the commotion and ran in the holding cell area with six other officers. They broke the fight up and took Denver out of the cell. Her nose was bloody from being punched in it so many times and her face was bright red. Other than that though, she was all right. If the officer's wouldn't have come when they did, it might have gotten ugly.

As she was sitting in another holding cell by herself, an officer called her name. "Denver Clark, there is someone here to see you."

Agent Kaplin was standing there with the officer. "Ms. Clark can you come with me?" he asked as the officer opened the cell door.

Denver stepped out of the cell and the officer quickly put cuffs on her. She then followed the agent to an interrogation room.

Once she was seated, Agent Kaplin began to speak. "Ms. Clark I am Special Agent Kapling and I'm sure you know why I'm here. I'm not going to beat around the bush with you. You are in deep shit right now and the only way you will be able get out of this is if you help me, help you," he said looking directly at Denver.

Denver just sat there staring at the wall and not saying a word. She was wondering what all he knew and what kind of time she would get, and most importantly was her sister okay.

"Can you please tell me where you got the checks from and where can we find the person or people behind them," Agent Kaplin said. He knew who the people were, but he didn't have real names or faces expect for one.

Denver looked at Agent Kaplin and was about to say something when they heard a knock at the door. The door opened and Louis Savino walked in confidently. "Don't say anything my dear. I am here now."

"Agent it is nice to see you again. I wish it was under different terms, but my client does not have anything to say to you. If you are charging her, then do it so we can get a bail hearing ASAP. If not, then please take these cuffs of her and let her go," Savino said, sounding all cocky.

Denver looked at Agent Kaplin and smiled, but that smile quickly disappeared when Agent Kaplin said, "Okay, book her on two counts of check fraud, theft by deception, access device fraud, and I will think of some more later," he told the lady officer who stood beside Denver.

She escorted Denver out to be booked. Agent Kaplin turned towards Savino and said, "Well counselor I don't think you will be wining this case. You should go spend your time trying to get some of the drug dealers off. You are way out of your league on this one.

"Savino just smiled at Agent Kaplin and then walked towards the door. When he turned the knob, he looked back at him and said, "We'll see who is out of their league. Good day Agent Kaplin." Savino walked out the door with a smile on his face.

Agent Kaplin stood there as his face turned red as hell thinking, *Who the fuck do he think he is?"*

CHAPTER 26

EJ had just gotten off the phone with Savino. They booked Denver and now she had to wait to see a judge for a bail hearing. He was going to try to get her Release on her Own Recognizance (ROR), but if he couldn't, then he would try to get her bail as low as possible.

EJ headed to the house on 56th Street to talk to Shannon. When he got there, there were a lot of people outside. He parked on the street and headed towards the house when he saw Lisa coming out of the house across the street.

"Where are you going in this weather?" EJ asked her.

"I'm about to go see my mom. Why are you asking? Are you gonna give me a ride?" she said coming across the street heading towards EJ.

"I have to take care of something right now, but if you give me a few minutes, I'll take you. It is cold as hell out here and it's starting to snow so just sit in my car and keep warm for a few minutes. I won't be in here too long," he said as he started walking back towards his car. He got in, started his car up, and put the heat on for her. Lisa hopped in and closed the door as he got out and walked back to the house to go talk to Shannon.

When he walked in the house, Shannon was laying on the couch talking on the phone. She told whomever she was talking to that, she would call them back. She got up and gave EJ a hug before sitting back down.

EJ sat next to her and took his coat off. "They are waiting for a bail hearing now. We should have her out by tonight," EJ said. "Now tell me what all went down at the bank because I need to figure some shit out."

Shannon told him everything that happened from the time they entered the bank until she walked out of the door. After she finished, EJ told her to get comfortable and he would be back soon. When he put his coat back on and walked to the door, he asked Shannon, "Do you need anything before I go?"

"No I'm just going to lay down and watch TV. Thank you though," Shannon said, giving him another hug.

"You can sleep in the bedroom. There is a king size bed and a 70' Plasma TV in there so get comfortable. I'll bring some food back or I will have some delivered," he said, walking out the door.

He got in the car and Lisa was sitting with her seat back listening to Keisha Cole on the radio. "So where does your mom live again?"

"She lives on 16th and Huntington Park," Lisa said relaxing, while listening to the music.

EJ pulled off headed for the expressway to drop Lisa off. He looked over at her and noticed that she had her coat off and her titties looked a little bit bigger now. He could see that she still had his name there. "Well at least I still have a place in your heart," EJ said smirking.

"Shut up boy. I'm not taking that off so you don't have to worry about that?" she said showing it to him.

EJ laughed at her comment. "So what are you doing with yourself now days?"

"Well I've been chilling. I've been trying to find a job. It's kind of hard though. I was working at the Purple Orchard on Jerry's Corner. The money was good, but I was tired of those thirsty ass niggas feeling all over me. It's not what I want to do for the rest of my life. Only one person has ever made me feel good with one touch, but that time has come and gone," she said staring at EJ.

EJ was shocked because he knew that she was talking about him. He turned to her and said, "Don't worry; I might have a job for you if you are interested."

"What do I have to do? Shit, I'll do almost anything right about now. My rent is past due for a month. I was thinking about going back to stripping," she said as she looked out the window.

"Well I'm in the check business and I could use you if you're not scared to cash a couple of them a week. The money is real good and you will make more than you ever would stripping," EJ said, waiting for her response.

She fell right for it. "Count me in. How much will I be making off of each check?"

"You will make anywhere from $2,000.00 to $10,000.00 a shot. It all depends on you," EJ said as he pulled up to her mom's house.

"Move down the street some so that we can talk for a minute," Lisa said.

EJ pulled down the street and parked at the corner. "I see you are starting to blossom from the last time that I saw you," he said, sipping on his soda.

Lisa started smiling. "I also got a clit ring too. Do you want to see it?"

She had always told EJ that she would get one of those. It was crazy that she really did it and she wanted to show it off. "Yeah, let me see," EJ said, watching her unbuckle her belt and pulling down her jeans and panties.

"See it? Ain't it pretty?" she asked showing off her prize.

"Yeah it is. Do you have better orgasms now that you have that?" EJ asked to see her response.

"Would you like to find out?" Lisa asked, seductively rubbing her fingers across her clit.

EJ really wanted to, but he had business in which to attend. He had to transfer all of his money to his offshore account. "I'll take your word for it. I will be calling you in about a week so be ready to go. Here is something to help you out while you are waiting," EJ said as he took an envelope out of the glove compartment and handed it to her. "It's two grand in there, so pay your rent and be ready when I call you."

She was fixing her clothes. After she was done, she gave him a hug and a kiss on the cheek. "Thank you and if you need anything, just call me," she said, getting out of the car and walking back towards her mom's house. EJ pulled off and headed back to Southwest Philly so he could take care of the accounts.

* * * *

Two weeks later, Denver was still in jail because she had violated her probation. She had a previous shoplifting charge from about a year ago in which she had received two years' probation. Now, because she had caught this new case, they had put a detainer on her. She was hoping that she beat the case because she didn't want to do any time.

She was sitting in her cell, listening to her Walkman when the CO came to her cell. "Ms. Clark, you have a visitor."

Denver sat her Walkman down and got herself together for her visit. She didn't know who was coming to see her this time. Shannon had just came to see her two days ago.

When she stepped in the visiting room, she was surprised when she saw EJ waiting for her. He hadn't come up since she had been in here. He sent her a couple of letters and he had put enough money on her books to feed the whole block. He held out his arms and she ran and jumped in them. Everybody was looking at them, so EJ gave them something in which to stare. He grabbed her ass and kissed her passionately.

"How's my girl holding up in here?" he asked letting her go.

"I'm good, but I wish I could go home. I need my hair and nails done," she said playfully.

"Well I got Savino working on your probation officer and hopefully your detainer will be lifted by next week," EJ said smiling.

"I hope so because this place sucks. I know that this is just a part of the game that we play, so I'm not stressing it. I'm a big girl so I can handle this. I just hope my sister will be okay because they have her ID too," Denver said seriously.

"Savino is working on her shit too. As a matter of fact, they should be at the police station now turning her in. She doesn't have a record so she will be out within a couple of hours. So I can tell you that she will be okay," he said.

Denver felt relieved that her little sister would be home and not in jail. She was staring at the couple taking pictures.

EJ noticed her staring and said, "Come on baby girl, let's go take a couple of pictures so you will have me to look at tonight."

"I wish I had more than just that picture," she said flirtatiously.

EJ laughed as they walked over to the picture man. They stood in front of the backdrop and EJ put Denver in front of him as he held her tight. She could feel his hard dick on her ass and instantly she got wet and her pussy started tingling.

After they took the pictures, they went back to their seats. They talked for about an hour before it was time for EJ to go.

"I will be here with a surprise when it's time for you to get out of here. No one else will be waiting but me. So I will see you next week, okay?" EJ said, giving her another hug and a longer than normal kiss. He cared about her, but he wasn't in love with her. No one had his heart, but his wife and son.

"Okay, I'll see you later. I will call you tonight if you're not with wifey," she said playfully.

"Girl you better call whenever you can. You know she is worried about you more than I am," he said, walking with her to the door that she through which had to leave. They said goodbye again and she left.

When EJ got to his car, he heard banging on the windows. When he looked up, he saw a women flashing their titties and trying to give him their inmate number by holding up a piece of paper in the window. He just laughed and jumped in his Bentley and pulled off. All the guards that were outside were looking at him wondering who he was with a car like that. He just nodded his head to the music and headed home.

* * * *

A week later as promised, Denver walked out of Riverview Women's Correctional Facility. She still had a court date set for next month, but at least she was out. As soon as she came out of the door, a stretched limo was waiting for her.

EJ was standing outside with his fur coat on because it was cold as hell out there. She walked over to him and gave him a hug. They jumped in the limo and pulled off.

"So how does it feel to be free for a while?" EJ asked as she sat the bag with her legal stuff in it down.

"You said you would have me out and you did. Thank you so much."

"You can change your clothes. I got you something to wear until you get home. That way you can throw that shit away," he said, passing her that bag that was sitting on the seat.

She started taking her clothes off and putting the tights on when she noticed EJ watching her. "What are you looking at? Can't a girl get dressed in private?" she said laughing.

EJ turned his head and closed his eyes. "Go ahead big head. I'm tired anyway," he said as he waited for her to get done.

"You know I was only playing with you. It ain't like you haven't seen this good-good before," she said grabbing his dick. "I see somebody misses me."

She unfastened his jeans and pulled his dick out. She started sucking it slowly. EJ leaned back and enjoyed the sensation until he came all in her mouth.

She swallowed it all and even licked the head until no more came out. "This is what I was missing. Now I need you to fuck the shit out of me before you take me home."

"You know I got you. Bring that ass over here," he said as Denver got on top of him and placed his still hard dick in her wet pussy. She came so fast that it felt like she came as soon as he put the head in. She was horny from being in jail so she rode his dick until she had multiple orgasms. By the time she got to her house, EJ had fucked her in every position he could in that limo. He dropped her off, went to the meeting house, and took a shower before heading home to his family.

CHAPTER 27

June 6, 2013

Chan was on his way home when he received a call from Ms. Cynthia. "Hey Ms. Cynthia, how are you doing? I just dropped the new locations off at your house, but you weren't there," Chan said.

"I had a meeting this morning, but I will check them out when I get home," she said, hanging up.

They had switched everything up. Every time they deposited a check, they would transfer it to another account so nothing would happen. They had now lost fifteen workers because, for some reason, the cops were now always one step ahead of them. It was as if they knew their every move. EJ and Chan suspected that someone was snitching, but they didn't know whom.

As Chan pulled up on 39th and Melon to meet one of his workers, he didn't notice the people sneaking up on his car. As soon as he went to open the door, a gun was in his face. "You know what the fuck it is! Give that shit up!"

Chan was scared because he never expected to be stuck up around his friend's aunt's house. He passed them the money and his watch that he had on.

After they got that, they took their hoods off. Chan couldn't believe who was robbing him. "What the hell are you doing? Why would you want to rob me?" Chan asked in shock.

"I need the money and this is personal. Since you saw our faces, I can't let you live," the robber said.

"Come on man, you don't have to do this. We can work something out," Chan said pleading for his life.

"I'm sorry."

BLOC! BLOC! BLOC! BLOC!

Gunfire was all that was heard as the bullets hit him in his chest and stomach.

Then the robbers ran around the corner to a car that was waiting for them and jumped in. The driver pulled off as if nothing had just happened.

When people heard the gunfire, they came out of their houses and looked to see what had just happened. When they saw the man sitting in his car with blood all over his body, they couldn't believe it.

"Call the cops!" someone yelled as they tried to help Chan, but it was too late. He was already dead.

* * * *

The death of Chan hit everybody hard, especially EJ and Wan. The cops thought that it was a robbery or drug deal gone badly. They were wondering why Chan was in that area in the first place being that he was an Asian American. That one thing alone had the cops puzzled.

EJ and Wan were trying to cope with the fact that their partner and friend was gone. "Damn, I should have went with him down there instead of letting him go by himself," Wan said, sitting on the couch.

"Then I would be burying two of my friends instead of one. You can't blame yourself for what some random asshole out there did to Chan. It's nobody's fault, but the person who pulled the trigger," EJ said, touching Wan on the shoulder.

They sat and talked for a couple of hours with Chan's wife. They told her that they would pay for the funeral arrangements. She was thankful that Chan had some good friends on his side.

As EJ was driving home, he was thinking about how everything seemed to be going in the wrong direction for him. He knew all good things would eventually end, but he didn't think that he would be losing so many people in the process.

Maria was gone and now Chan. Ed was on the run for not showing up to court. He didn't care because he knew they wouldn't come for him unless he got knocked for something else. He also lost a lot of workers because someone was tipping the cops off about his operation.

One thing about him though, he wouldn't let that stop the show. He was determined to get rich by any means necessary. Since the check business was hot right now, he decided to do something else. He had never done this before, but he needed money to keep flowing. He was going to get Ed to find a contact so that they could make some money. They would still do the check thing, but it just wouldn't be so often. They still had the cops on their ass so he really had to slow it down.

"Yo, Ed we need to find a contact and fast," EJ said, talking to Ed on the phone.

"You sure you want to do this? I haven't played around with that stuff since my mom's situation," Ed said.

"Well it's time to get back in the game. I'm still going to sell the credit cards and I will still be doing the checks. I just want the extra money to come in so we can still reach our goal," EJ said.

"Okay well I'll call Tuck and see what's what out there," Ed said, hanging up.

Tuck was the man to see now. Ever since Ed had turned his business over to him, he had North Philly, South Philly, and West Philly on smash. He was damn near supplying the whole Philly area. The people that Ed introduced him to had the purest coke that money could buy, even though it was stepped on one or two times.

When EJ got home, he went in the living room and gave his wife a kiss. "Where is my little man at?" he asked.

"Ziaire is with my mom for the night. I thought we needed some alone time," she said seductively.

"That would be real nice," he said feeling her pussy through her panties. She opened her legs and enjoyed the foreplay.

"Go get the Jacuzzi ready and I'll be up in a minute. I just have to check on our offshore account," he said booting up the laptop.

He pulled up his Cayman Island account to see what his balance was. Ever since a lot of shit had went down, he had switched to the Atlantic International Bank of Belize. He didn't have to worry about this bank. Whenever anything goes wrong, they would notify him and transfer his money into a new account within the bank.

When he pulled up his balance, a big smile spread across his face. He was almost there. He closed the laptop and went into the kitchen. He grabbed some whipped cream and strawberries out of the refrigerator. Then he went upstairs to join Yahnise for a night of love making that the both of them so desperately needed.

* * * *

Agent Kaplin and Detective Harris had received a call from their CI informing them that some things were about to change. They didn't know what so they decided to wait it out and just listen to the wiretaps. Agent Kaplin was shocked when he heard EJ tell Ed to set up a drug connect for them. He now knew who EJ was thanks to the information that he had received from the CI. In fact, he knew who they all were now. Chan was deceased so he was out of the equation.

Their CI was becoming a very valuable asset to them. With all of the stuff, they had now and the testimony from the CI, they could put them away for a long time, but Agent Kaplin wanted more and he intended on getting it.

He was listening to the surveillance tapes when his boss called him into his office. He got up and went to see what his boss was going to fuss about this time.

When he stepped in his office, his boss was waiting on him. "Have a seat Keith. We need to discuss a few things," he said.

From the look on his face, Agent Kaplin could tell that it was about to be some bullshit. He sat down and waited for his boss to begin.

"Where is John? He should be here for this also," his boss said taking his glasses off and sitting them on his desk.

"The last I checked, he was on his way here so that we could go over the wiretaps," Agent Kaplin said.

"That's what this meeting is about. I'm going to terminate the wiretaps after this week. We've invested too much money in them and they are not using their phones to say anything incriminating. Everything you have on them so far has come from the CI. Whoever this person is, their testimony alone will cook them," his boss said to him.

"But sir we are getting close. They just said something on their yesterday about getting drugs from somebody. We need that tap to get them," Agent Kaplin pleaded desperately.

"Well, I'm giving you until the end of the week and then it's over," his boss said trying to be a little reasonable. "I'm sorry it has to be this way, but I'm getting cursed out from above so you know that shit goes downhill."

Agent Kaplin knew he was right, but he still was pissed. He also knew that he could get them just off of his CI's testimony alone. Agent Kaplin left his bosses office and walked back to his desk. Detective Harris was walking up as he sat down.

He filled Detective Harris in on everything that had went down at the meeting. He even told him that it was time to start turning shit up so that they would be able to nail them soon.

"Let's start from the beginning by looking at all of the checks that have been cashed and the names of the people that were involved,"

Detective Harris said.

"Call the CI and let him know that we need more information on EJ and Wan. We also want to know what is the main bank that he is using and everything else that he can tell us about him. Try to get anything that will give us a strong case," Agent Kaplin said as he began pulling up all of the profiles of the people he had. He especially paid close attention to Mr. Edward Young who he had in the system now thanks to his arrest.

"It's just a matter of time before I have you and your fucking crew where y'all belong," Agent Kaplin said, pointing to Ed's profile.

Later That Day

Ms. Cynthia had started using heroin more and more lately. She would always get her friend Cathy to purchase it and together they would stay at Ms. Cynthia's house and shoot up. It became so bad that she had quit her job. She told Ed that she quit so she could be able to help him more. She was becoming more and more involved since Chan had been killed.

What they didn't notice about her so far was her weight. She had started to lose a few pounds that she claimed happened from going to the gym. She had her excuses ready just in case somebody noticed it.

She was in the backseat of the car with her legs in the air getting dicked down. After the man bust his nut in the condom, he pulled up his pants and got back in the front seat.

"Damn, that dick gets better every time we fuck," Ms. Cynthia said as she pulled her skirt down and got in the passenger seat.

"I'm glad you liked it. Now maybe we can start doing it in the house instead of the car. I wish I could take you to my house, but my wife would kill the both of us," he said.

"I don't want my kids in my business and they sure wouldn't like the fact that I'm fucking a married cop," she said.

Ms. Cynthia and Detective Harris had been fucking around ever since that day that she played with her pussy in the car for him. He liked her because she had a bad body and since he knew she was on that shit, he had a little control over her. He would meet up with her once a week and they would have sex. He would also give her a little bit of drugs that he had taken from the evidence room.

He didn't let Agent Kaplin know any of his personal business, because he knew that he wouldn't approve of what he was doing. He loved his wife, but with Ms. Cynthia, it was the thrill of knowing that he was fucking one of his suspects mother. He was just hoping that it wouldn't affect their relationship when he put her kids behind bars.

CHAPTER 28

E d was chilling in Scooter's on 38th and Lancaster Avenue watching the NBA Finals. The Miami Heat were playing the San Antonio Spurs and the Spurs were digging in their asses. Ed had more than enough drinks tonight so he was about to head home. "You're not staying for the rest of the game?" the cute bartender asked.

"Naw, its past my curfew. My wife is already tripping about me coming home late every night. I'll see you next week, though," Ed said heading out the door. He walked towards his car not paying any attention to his surroundings or the black Toyota Camry sitting in the Unite Bank parking lot.

As he got to his car, something just didn't feel right. He looked around, but he didn't see anything that looked suspicious. He unlocked his door and sat in the driver's seat. He bent down, grabbed his 40 caliber from under the seat, and put it on his lap. Just when he was about to start his car up, a girl he was fucking called his name. He stepped out of his car and slowly walked over to her.

"Hey Ed, why haven't you called me in a long time?" the girl questioned him with her hand on her hip.

"What's up Tara? You are looking good tonight. Where are you coming from dressed like that?" he said, looking at the tight ass dress she was wearing that hugged all of her curves.

"I'm on my way home from a friend's party. Can I get a ride if you are not too busy?" she asked.

Ed wanted some of that pussy so he said, "Sure, I'll take you home. Let me cut my car on so it can cool down some of this heat while I grab me a Dutch and a condom," he smirked.

She looked at him as if he was crazy. It was hot as hell out there and they both were sweating. Ed went to hit the automatic starter on his car and his car blew up, knocking him and the girl to the ground.

The loud explosion caused some of the windows in Scooter's to break along with some of the cars that were near his.

Ed looked up in total shock as his Benz was engulfed in flames. "Are you okay?" he asked the girl helping her up.

"Yes, but why did your car just do that?" she asked as they stood there and watched his car burn up.

As soon as he was about to say something, he saw a Toyota Camry pull off out the lot, as if someone was chasing them. He thought he had seen that car before, but he wasn't sure.

"I don't know what the fuck is going on, but I'm damn sure going to find out," Ed said as he waited for the fire trucks that he heard coming.

* * * *

EJ hung up the phone with Ed and just sat there wondering why somebody would try to kill Ed. First Chan, and now Ed. Something wasn't adding up and he needed to see who was next. They were back in the game now thanks to Tuck. He gave them a whole block and it was doing crazy numbers. He figured that once they reached their goal that they could fall back and get some properties like those that they had planned.

He tried to call Denver a couple of times, but he only got her voicemail. He then tried to call Tiffany and Shannon, but he got the same results. He left a message on all of their phones hoping that at least one of them would call him back tonight.

* * * *

Denver was over at some dudes house that she had met about a month ago. He had invited her to a home cooked meal. When she stepped in the apartment, she could smell the aroma of baked ziti and it made her mouth water.

"Damn that smells so good. I see you can cook a little bit. Now if it taste half as good as it smells, you will have me sold," she said, sitting on the loveseat.

"Would you like something to drink?" he asked as he poured himself a drink.

"I sure do. Do you have any Cîroc?" she asked.

"One glass of Cîroc coming right up," he said making her a drink.

He came and sat down on the couch next to her. Then he passed her the drink as he sipped on his. Denver swallowed her drink as if it was water. "Damnnnn, slow down baby! If you keep drinking like that you might not be going home tonight," he said with a smirk on his face.

"That's my favorite drink and don't worry about me. I can hold my liquor," she said, handing him her glass for a refill.

As she was sitting there waiting for him to come back with her refill, she started feeling dizzy. He walked back in the room and looked at her holding her head. "I see that it's working," he said.

Denver looked at him, but she was seeing triples. "What have you done to me, you fucking bastard?" she said slurring her words.

At that moment, someone walked out of the bedroom and came over to where Denver was seated. Denver looked at the person and tried to speak, but nothing came out.

"Don't worry; you will be dead in the next few minutes. I'm sorry that you have to die like this, but you are in my way to rising to the top with EJ. I took out Chan and I tried to take out Ed, but he move at the right time. I won't make that same mistake with you or your sister," the person said.

Denver tried to jump up and swing at the mention of her sister's name, but she fell straight to the floor. She could no longer keep her eyes open as darkness started fading in. She couldn't believe that this person that she was staring at used to be her friend. She laid there fighting it, but she finally gave into the darkness that took her to eternity.

"Clean this mess up and don't let anybody see you. Soon I will be in charge and we will be making all of the money," they said as they left the apartment.

One Week Later

Denver's decomposed body turned up in Fairmount Park. A couple of joggers found her while going on their early morning jog. Everyone was really fucked up about that. EJ wanted to shut everything down until he found out what was going on. He still had a bunch of money that he needed to transfer to his offshore accounts. He decided that no one could be trusted so he installed hidden cameras in the meeting house hoping that whoever was killing all of his people would slip up.

EJ had a private investigator follow a different employee every week to see if they had any changes in their patterns. Truth be told, he thought they would try to get him or his family next. He knew only one person knew where his new home was and that was Ed so in his mind, he thought they were safe.

There were two problems going on at the same time and he had to figure out who was behind both of them. One was, people were getting killed in his group, and his second problem was that he had a mole that was assisting the police in locking up all of his people. Altogether, he had to get this operation under control and fast!

He was at home hanging out with his wife and son today. He had decided to take a day off from running around. He planned on just staying at home chilling with his family and trying to figure out some shit. Yahnise was giving Ziaire a bath so that they could go over Nyia's house for a while. She felt like EJ needed some time alone so she wanted to give it to him.

* * * *

Detective Harris and Agent Kaplin were at the Federal Building frustrated because another one of their suspects had been killed. They didn't know what was going on, but they sure wasn't going to just sit around and wait for someone else to get killed. They started building their case.

"Call our CI and let him know that the time has come to start setting our plan into motion. We need that evidence so that we can get these assholes off of the street," Agent Kaplin said to Detective Harris.

He looked at his partner in agreement and said, "I'll call right now."

The CI had given them a lot of detailed information, but the District Attorney wanted more. She was a tough Son of a Bitch (SOB) and she had a conviction rate of 86% so you best believe when she came, she came correct.

After Detective Harris hung the phone up, he looked at his partner and said, "Everything is going according to plan. We will have what we need soon."

"Good because I'm sick and tired of this shit already. It's time to move on to some different shit. Plus I need a damn vacation," Agent Kaplin said, sitting up in his chair typing something on the computer.

They spent the next couple of hours putting everything together that they had. Through all the months of gathering Intel, they were able to gather more information than they would have ever thought. Now they just had to put everything in a report format. Both of them had their work cut out for them. With all of that and their CI's testimony, they were sure to get a conviction.

* * * *

Wan was picking up the last of the money from their last package. He pulled up to the house on 19th and Mountain Street in South Philly. He called the girl on his cell and told her that he was outside. There was a car parked at the corner in which he didn't pay any attention. Little did he know it was the same Toyota Camry from the hit on Ed.

When the girl came out, she jumped in the car with Wan. "I took my money out and left yours in there and so did my friend. It's $50,000.00 in this bag. It's $25,000.00 from each of us. If you need us again this week, just let me know."

"I sure will and don't leave that money in that account to long. There's a lot of shit going on right now. Be careful and tell your friend the same thing," Wan said as the girl exited the car.

He pulled off heading back to Southwest to drop the money off and then go home. He noticed the Camry following him, but he didn't think anything of it. He stopped at a gas station on 21st and Jackson to get some gas.

When Wan exited the car, he noticed the Camry pulling across the street. The windows were tinted so he couldn't tell who was in the car. He seen a young boy pumping different people's gas so he called him over to his car. "Yo, do you want to make a couple of dollars? If you do, then pump my gas for me," Wan said as he went to pay the cashier.

Wan watched from the window as the young boy pumped his gas. When he was done, Wan left the store and went back to his car. As he sat in his car, he took his Glock 19 out of the center console and cocked it back. He then sat it under his leg as he noticed the passenger exit the car. When he saw who it was, he let his guard down shortly. As soon as he did that, he saw the driver step out and both of them started firing at Wan's car.

BLOC! BLOC! BLOC! BLOC! BLOC! POP! POP! POP! POP! POP! POP!

Gunfire was all that could be heard as Wan ducked out the car and took cover.

He started firing back which caused the two assailants to retreat. He kept firing until his gun was empty.

BLOC! BLOC! BLOC! BLOC! BLOC! BLOC! BLOC! BLOC! BLOC!

He immediately reloaded and when he did, he heard sirens and then a car screeching away in a hurry. Wan jumped in his car and went to start it up when he noticed the young boy who had just pumped his gas laying on the ground.

He jumped out of his car and ran over to the boy. He was bleeding from his stomach. Wan knew he needed to get out of there, but he couldn't just leave the boy laying there. Before he had time to think, the cops were already pulling up.

Wan put his hands up in the air as the cops aimed their guns at him. "Don't move! Keep your hands where I can see them!" one of the cops yelled.

Two other cops came running up to Wan and put handcuffs on him. They escorted him to one of the patrol cars.

Wan wasn't even worried about getting locked up. He was worried about the kid that had got shot. He was in a daydream until he saw a cop pull the gun out of his car. *"Oh shit!"* Wan said to himself.

He forgot that he was also shooting. He sat there wondering did his gun fire the bullet that had hit the kid. "Please God, let that kid be okay," he said out loud as a cop got in the car and drove him to the 1st District Police Station on 24th and Wolf Street.

One thing Wan did realize was, now he knew who had shot Chan and killed Denver. He couldn't wait to call EJ to inform him. He knew his friend was going to be pissed at the news, but he had to tell him.

* * * *

When EJ hung up the phone, he was in total shock of the news he had just received. He couldn't believe that someone would betray him like this. The whole time that EJ was working with this person, come to find out it was all a plot to get to the top.

He went into his closet and grabbed his bulletproof vest. Then he opened up his safe and grabbed his 40 caliber along with two extra clips. When he went downstairs, Yahnise was cooking and she only looked up at him for a brief moment. "What's wrong now, baby? Please, don't say someone else was murdered," she said, walking over to him.

She had seen that look on his face before, so she knew that either someone had died or was about to die. "I have to go to Philly for a little while. I don't know when I will be back, but you know what to do if anything happens to me," he said as he kissed his wife goodbye.

Tears started falling from her eyes as EJ walked out the door, jumped in his car, and headed for Philly. She wasn't worried about EJ because she knew that Wan and Ed had his back. What she was worried about was what if they all got locked up in the process. Yahnise didn't want and couldn't imagine raising their son all by herself. She needed her husband there with them. She loved him more than anything in this whole world did so she went over and knelt down by the couch. She prayed to God as if the world was ending, asking God to return him safely.

* * * *

EJ had called everybody over to the meeting house. If they were in the middle of doing something, they had to stop and get there immediately. He made it clear to everyone that whomever missed this meeting, he was going to clear their accounts out. He had access to everyone's bank accounts because he transferred the money to them every time they completed a job.

This day would be different though. He had just came from visiting Wan in CFCF and Wan had told him everything that had happened. He also told him about the people involved with the hit on Denver and Chan, and the attempted hit on Ed and himself.

Once everybody was seated, he began, "I know everyone is wondering why I called this emergency meeting and threatened to clear out their accounts if you didn't show up. Well it seems that we have a problem within our circle. It seems that we have some snakes and rats amongst us," EJ said standing in front of the window. Everyone was looking around at each other wondering who it could be. People were getting nervous while others just sat there expressionless.

EJ continued, "Did you know that in the wilderness, snakes eat rats and hawks eat snakes. Well guess what people, I am that hawk looking for its prey. Today the line has been crossed and the predator has found its prey," EJ said as he walked over to where Ed was sitting.

"I have to say that I honestly didn't see this coming. We shared a lot of time together. I did everything in my power to make you rich and you still crossed me. You killed people that meant a lot to me and now you actually had the nerve to come here to this meeting instead of running away for your life," EJ said as tears ran down his face.

Ed just sat there with his game face on. While everybody watched EJ talk to his friend, Ed just sat there shaking his head. He just couldn't believe what he was hearing. Tamara had come with Ed, because he was a part of the organization too. She was the accountant along with Shannon. She became teary eyed just listening to EJ talk to Ed. Tamara couldn't believe what she was hearing and she was hoping that it wasn't true.

EJ then turned around and said, "If you don't confess in front of everybody right now and tell me who was involved, I will blow your fucking brains out of the back of your head." He turned back around aiming his gun at Jamie's head.

Everyone was confused for a moment looking from EJ to Jamie waiting for an explanation. "This is the person behind the murders of Chan and Denver. She also tried to kill Ed and Wan," EJ said.

At that moment, Ed pulled his 40 caliber that he had tucked beside him out and pointed it at Jamie's side. He knew what was going on the whole time. EJ and him had talked earlier about it and he wanted to kill her on site, but EJ had told him to wait until they had both of them together. That's why he had sat next to her on the couch.

"Her and her little boyfriend Ronald are the culprits behind this whole thing. We went looking for the nigga, but all of his stuff was already gone," Ed said poking her in the side with his hammer (gun) hoping she did something to make him pull the trigger.

The whole time, she thought EJ was talking about Ed. She had a smirk on her face because she thought she had gotten away with it. Shannon jumped up and tried to hit her, but EJ caught her. "Let me fuck this bitch up! She killed my sister! Let me go! Let me go!" she kept screaming.

"You have to calm down right now. You are too emotional right now. Go and cool off and let us handle this. Matter of fact, this meeting is over. Everybody go ahead and go home," EJ said still holding Shannon.

Everybody started leaving out the door when Tiffany stayed seated. "I want to help kill this bitch and her nigga for what they have done to my best friend," she said still seated.

After EJ walked Shannon to her car, he came back in and locked the door behind him. "Now why the fuck did you kill my friend?" he asked standing in front of Jamie.

"I didn't want to do it EJ, I swear. Ronald made me do it. This was his entire fault. Please don't kill me," Jamie said, pleading for her life.

"This is what we are gonna do. You are gonna call your man and tell him to meet us at your apartment on 49th and Spruce. If everything goes alright, I will think about letting you live," he said passing her the cell phone out of her purse.

Jamie called Ronald and he answered on the third ring. "Hey baby, what's up?" she said while EJ, Ed, and Tiff listened to him on speaker phone.

"I just got out the shower. Let's go try to catch that nigga's wife while she is over her sister's house today. If we kill her and the boy, he will turn everything over to us," Ronald said with no idea who was listening.

EJ controlled his anger as he listened to that nigga plot to kill his family.

"Meet me at my apartment in thirty minutes. I have something to show you," Jamie said to Ronald.

"I'll be there soon. Just be ready to give me some of that pussy when I get there and then we'll be on our way to take care of our business," he said ending the call.

"Now what do you wanna do?" Ed said still aiming the gun at Jamie's head.

"Let's get to the apartment and wait for this clown to arrive. I have something special planned for him when he gets there," EJ said as they walked out the door and got into the Denali that EJ had purchased earlier from a chop shop out North.

* * * *

They were sitting in the apartment waiting for Ronald to get there. They had stripped Jamie down to her panties and bra and had her tied to the chair.

Ed was peeking out the window when he saw Ronald pull up and park. "He's here," he said, pulling out his gun. EJ did the same as they both went and stood by the door.

Jamie lived on the first floor so it wasn't long before Ronald knocked on the door. As soon as EJ opened the door, Ed snatched Ronald into the apartment and smacked him with his gun. Ronald fell on his knees holding his head.

"Get the fuck up, you bitch ass nigga," Ed said, pulling him up to his feet.

When he saw EJ, he knew nothing good was going to come out of this situation. He didn't know what they knew so he played dumb. "What is this about, EJ? I didn't do anything," he said.

"You can cut the bullshit games out. We heard your little conversation with your bitch. Did you really think that you would get away with this nigga?" EJ said, hitting Ronald with a two piece that crumbled him to the floor.

"Strip nigga!" Ed said to Ronald as he was laying on the floor in pain.

"Come on man, please... I didn't mean anything by that. We were only going to hold them until we got ransom money. Please don't kill me. It was her idea," Ronald said, knowing he wasn't getting out of this alive.

EJ looked at Ed and Tiff. "That's funny because she said the same shit, but yet and still both of y'all agreed to harm my family. I don't want to hear anything else from you. Tie this nigga up with this bitch," EJ said as he grabbed the bag that he brought with him.

After Ed tied Ronald up in a chair beside Jamie, he looked at EJ. "What are we going to do with them now?" he said.

EJ smirked at him and pulled out a can filled with acid and passed it to Tiffany. "Here you go beautiful. Have fun with this bitch while Ed and I have some fun of our own with him.

Tiffany walked over to Jamie and stood in front of her with the can. She started crying and struggling to say something, but nobody could hear her because her mouth was gagged.

"Don't cry now bitch! You didn't cry when you killed my friend," she said as she threw the acid all over her body and face. The acid started eating her alive from her skin all the way down to her bones. It was a horrifying sight.

EJ pulled out the sledge hammers he had in the bag. He passed Ed one and he walked over to Ronald. In one quick swing, he hit Ronald in the knee cap breaking it instantly. Ronald had a muffled scream that no one could hear.

"My turn," Ed said as he hit him in his other knee with the hammer. He was in so much pain that he went into shock.

They were nowhere near done as they did the same thing to Jamie. They tortured them for an hour until they got tired. EJ, Ed, and Tiffany did all types of shit to Ronald and Jamie. Jamie's insides were on the floor from the acid eating her up.

EJ then took out his 40 caliber and put a silencer on it. He walked up to both of the bodies and put four bullets in each of their heads.

"Call your cleanup crew to come take care of this and I'll get up with y'all later," EJ said to Ed as he walked towards the door.

"Take my truck. I have someone picking me up," he said and left.

CHAPTER 29

October 5, 2013

It had been months since the incident with Jamie and Ronald. Since they have been gone, business has been crazy. They were making more money now than they had ever made and it was mostly from drugs. It's crazy because EJ never wanted to go that route. When the check scam got hot, he had to do something. His credit card business had slowed up to because he didn't want to take any chances on getting caught.

He was sitting in his office in the basement of his home, talking to his best friend and partner about his come up in the game. "Damn dog, we finally did it," Ed said as he poured himself a drink. He came over and sat in the chair in front of the desk that EJ was sitting at. "You said that we would be millionaires by the time we turned thirty and we hit that mark already at the age of twenty-two. I didn't think it would happen to us this fast in the game, but you had a vision and we turned it into a successful enterprise."

EJ sat there with a cool smirk on his face admiring what his best friend was saying. They had checked their overseas accounts thirty minutes ago and realized that they had reached the millionaire mark. Although it had come at a deadly price, it was well worth it. They were finally living the lifestyle of the rich and famous and to them; they were on top of the world.

"Yeah dawg, we have come a long way from living in the projects, playing with carts and shit, dry humping on girls, and pretending that we were driving cars. Now we are actually doing that shit, from driving luxury cars to fucking some of the baddest bitches. We are also living in some exotic ass houses," EJ said, while looking at a picture of him and his wife Yahnise and their son Ziaire.

He put the picture down, got up, walked over to the bar, and poured himself some soda. Then he went over to where Ed was, "We have to find out who this mole is in our organization and eliminate them. We've been lucky to make it this far after all the shit that has happened and we have to be even more cautious," EJ said to his friend.

"I know what you're saying and I have people on it as we speak. When they tell me something, I won't hesitate to put two bullets between their eyes, Ed said while pulling out his 40 caliber from his shoulder holster and cocking it back.

"But for now I have to get home before Tamara tries to kill a nigga," he said, walking towards the steps with EJ right behind him. They both knew that business was now over for the night. It was time to get home and get some much needed rest. Tomorrow everyone would be going to Ed's mothers surprise birthday party. What they didn't know was that it could be the last day of their freedom.

* * * *

The next day was hectic for everybody involved in setting up for the surprise birthday party for Ed's mom. It was a special occasion because not only was it her 40th birthday, it had been a year that she had been clean, or so they thought. She had been hiding her addiction very well. She had another dark secret that she hoped wouldn't come to the light also.

It was about an hour before Yahnise and Tamara was supposed to bring Ms. Cynthia to Warm Daddy's on Columbus Boulevard. They were at the Gallery buying her some clothes. Even though Ed always made sure she always had money, it was her birthday so they were treating her. They were in the food court section of the mall sitting at a table talking, trying to rest for a few minutes.

They had hit almost every store they could picking up stuff for Ms. Cynthia. Now they needed a break. "So do you think you have enough Ms. Cynthia," Tamara asked, looking at all the bags sitting around the table.

"Shit, a woman can never have enough clothes. Shit, I think I need some more," Ms. Cynthia said as they all started laughing.

"Well we have to be somewhere in about an hour, so you're going to have to come with us," Yahnise said, looking at her watch.

"After all this stuff y'all bought me, you can take me to a strip club and I wouldn't complain, she said.

"We know you wouldn't complain. You would be too busy watching all of those dicks in your face," Tamara said smiling.

"You know it," Ms. Cynthia said, slapping hands with both girls.

"Okay, let's get out of here so we can handle our business," Yahnise said as they all got up and started grabbing bags.

Just as they started walking, Ms. Cynthia's cell phone rang. When she looked and seen who it was, she told the girls, "Excuse me for a minute while I use the restroom."

Tamara and Yahnise waited by the door as she ran in to answer her cell phone. After about three minutes, she came back out and they all headed for the car.

* * * *

Ed and EJ were at the restaurant making sure everything was ready. They had a live band and everything. There were so many people there that they didn't have enough tables and chairs for everybody.

Ed was on the phone with Tamara, and after he hung up he said, "Everybody get in their places. They just parked and they are walking up right now."

Tamara and Yahnise let Ms. Cynthia walk in first and as soon as she stepped in the door, all that was heard was everyone yelling, "SURPRISE! HAPPY BIRTHDAY!"

Ms. Cynthia was so happy that she started crying. Ed and EJ walked over to her and gave her a big hug and kiss. "Happy Birthday Mom," Ed said.

"This is the best surprise ever. How were you able to keep it a secret so long," she said to her son.

"Well, we planned it three days ago. Now come on and have a seat. We have some people that want to sing to you," Ed said, leading her to a seat.

When everyone was seated, that could sit down, the music started playing, and Jagged Edge walked up and started singing. *"I got so much love for you in these arms. Don't you know that you are my good luck charm...?"*

Ms. Cynthia couldn't believe that her favorite group was here live and in person. She was in total shock and she was truly enjoying the show.

Everyone was having a good time. After they sung Happy Birthday to Ms. Cynthia, she cut her four layer cake that Tamara had purchased from Tiffany's a week ago.

They had cake and ice-cream with plenty of liquor. EJ went up to the mike to give a speech. "Can I have everyone's attention please," he said as the crowd quieted down and looked towards the stage where he was.

"I would like to thank everyone for coming out today to celebrate my step-mom's birthday and one year anniversary of being clean." He looked at Ms. Cynthia and then continued, "Mom, the past is where you learned your lesson. The future is where you apply that lesson, so don't give up in the middle. We all love you here and wish you the best. Enjoy life to the fullest and may all your wishes come true," EJ said, raising his glass of orange and cranberry juice in the air. Everybody else raised their drinks and saluted Ms. Cynthia. She was in tears at this moment.

Ed and everybody else came over, hugged, and kissed her as they enjoyed the party.

It was now 10:00 at night, and everything was dying down. Everyone had started to leave and the few people who were left were helping load all of Ms. Cynthia's presents into the Denali. Her phone started ringing and she excused herself and stepped out of sight to answer it.

EJ and Ed had finished loading up the truck when the girls walked up. "Well, I'm outta here. I'll catch you guys tomorrow," EJ said, giving Tamara a kiss and hugging Ed.

He and Yahnise walked towards his car so they could go home to their son. They had asked Mira to watch Ziaire tonight so they could come out to the party.

Ed waited for his mom to get in the truck and he and Tamara took her home. He really hoped that she had enjoyed herself because they had spent a lot of money to get Jagged Edge to perform for them. At the end of the day, it was well worth it just to see his mom happy.

* * * *

Over at the Federal Building, Agent Kaplin, Detective Harris, and a group of officers and agents were sitting in a conference room. ready to take down some suspects.

"My CI has informed me that everybody will be at their own houses tonight. So we will hit every one of them at the same time," Agent Kaplin said, looking at the group. He then continued, "I will lead a group out to Pottstown for Eric Johnson, AKA EJ, Detective Harris will lead a group over to Paulsboro, NJ for Edward Young, AKA Ed, Tom you will pick up Wan Lee, and Liz you will pick up Shannon Clark and Tiffany Green. Each one of you will have a Federal Agent with you because you will be crossing state lines. I have someone calling right now to give y'all jurisdiction and you will have local and state enforcement there to assist you in the arrest. Make sure you take all of the precautions because they can be armed and dangerous," Agent Kaplin said.

"I want you to also be aware that Eric has a little boy in there so watch where you shoot if you have to," Detective Harris said to Agent Kaplin.

"Okay, let's load up. We will go in at approximately 2:00 a.m. I will give the signal via radio. Everyone be safe and come back in one piece," Agent Kaplin said as they all headed out the door.

They had gathered so much intel from the CI that they were ready to bring them in. Over the last few months, their informant had been calling them with tips about everything from drugs to credit cards. Since it was a joint effort, the Feds let the state be the one to prosecute them. Therefore, this was Detective Harris moment to stardom and he was going to cash in on it.

* * * *

Ed was lying in bed with Tamara watching a movie on TV. They had just got finished making love and they both were exhausted. He looked over at his wife and said, "Do you still want that family now?"

She sat up and looked at him. "Are you serious, baby?"

"Yes, I think it's about time to bring a new life into the world. You're not going anywhere and I sure as hell ain't going anywhere," he said, smiling at her.

"Well in that case, I say we start right now," Tamara said as she started massaging Ed's dick trying to bring him back to life.

"If that's what you want," Ed said playfully getting on top of her as he felt his man coming to life.

* * * *

Yahnise was upstairs sleep and EJ was downstairs on the computer seeing how much drug money Savino his lawyer had washed up and transferred to his account.

Ziaire had stayed the night with Mira at Nyia's house because it was late when EJ and Yahnise had got home. In addition, he was already asleep so they didn't want to disturb him.

After he seen how much money was in his account, he made a mental note to thank his lawyer tomorrow, and to transfer it to his offshore account. His lawyer was as loyal as they came. Whatever he said he would do, he did it. He had been washing EJ and Ed's money for several years now.

He was a gambling man, so he was always at the casino, race track, boxing matches, etc. He took EJ's money so he didn't have to spend his. It was a win-win situation for him. They really didn't care because if he lost it, they could make it right back. He didn't have a care in the world.

He shut his computer off and went upstairs to join his wife in bed. He decided that tomorrow he would take his son to the New York Giant's game. They were playing the Eagles for the number one spot in the division.

* * * *

Shannon and Tiffany had an apartment on Broad and Cumberland that they shared. They both were enrolled in Temple University, paying their own tuition. They had both went to Ed's mom's party and then came home and fell asleep studying for a test that they had on Monday. They had no idea that there was about fifteen cops outside in all black waiting to arrest them.

* * * *

Wan's place was in Upper Darby. He stayed there with his girlfriend. They had been living together for four years now, and he still wouldn't marry her yet. He had told her to wait until New Year's and it would happen. He was in his basement working out with the Chinese stars and swords. He was good at Martial Arts. He was even thinking about opening up his own gym one day, but until then he was cool with working out in his own basement. He had been out on bail because the bullets that shot the kid didn't match his gun. He was thankful to know that the kid was in stable condition now.

* * * *

It was now 1:55 a.m. and Agent Kaplin got on his radio, "Alpha one to Alpha 2, 3, and 4, are all units ready to go?" he asked.

"Alpha two ready," Detective Harris said.

"Alpha three ready," Tom said.

"Alpha four ready," Elizabeth said.

"Okay, in sixty seconds everyone move in as swiftly and quietly as possible. All communication is shut down for now until 2:10 a.m. Let's make our bosses proud ladies and gentleman. Out," he said, turning his radio off. The time had come for him and he was smiling the whole way.

* * * *

EJ had just laid down when his alarm went off. He jumped up gabbing his 40 caliber from out the dresser drawer. "What's wrong baby," Yahnise said, looking at him.

"Somebody's trying to break in," he said, turning the monitor on.

Yahnise ran to the closet and pulled out the AR-15 from the floor safe. She was riding with her husband.

EJ watched the monitor and couldn't believe what he was seeing. "Oh shit baby! It's the cops! Put all the guns back in the safe!" he said, passing her his 40 caliber.

She put the guns up and put on some tights and a shirt while EJ threw on some basketball shorts and a t-shirt.

All of a sudden, there was a big bang on the door. All that was heard was about a dozen people running up the stairs screaming, "Police! Come out with your hands up!"

EJ yelled, "I'm in the bedroom and we are unarmed."

The cops ran in pointing their weapons at EJ and Yahnise. "Put your hands on your heads and don't move!"

They cuffed Yahnise and EJ while the other cops searched the house. "Do you have anything in here that we should know about?" Agent Kaplin asked, walking in the door.

"No, so what the fuck are you hear for? I hope you have a warrant, you piece of shit!" EJ said sounding extremely angry.

Agent Kaplin showed him the warrant and told his men to keep searching the house.

* * * *

At that same time over in Jersey, Detective Harris and his team were raiding Ed's crib. They caught him sleeping. When he opened his eyes, there were about ten guns pointed at him and Tamara. "Move and die motherfucker!" Detective Harris said as the other cops cuffed Ed and Tamara. Ed had his Glock 19 sitting on the nightstand.

Detective Harris took it and put it in an evidence bag. "What do we have here? You are a wanted man, my friend," he said, looking at Ed.

"You are under arrest for possession of a firearm. Get this piece of shit out of here and take her too while we search this place. Don't forget to read him his rights and show him the search warrant also," Detective Harris said as they started to ransack the place.

* * * *

Over on Broad Street, Tiffany and Shannon were taken into custody with no problem. In Upper Darby though, it was a different story. When the cops tried to take Wan into custody, he started fighting with them. They beat him up so bad that he had to go to the hospital and get stitches.

The best part was that he didn't go alone. Five cops went with rib injuries and one had a broken arm. Wan didn't like cops ever since they had killed his cousin in South Philly when he was only fourteen years old. That hate grew more and more as he got older.

* * * *

It was now 3:30 a.m. and Agent Kaplin was just leaving EJ's house. They had nothing, but the safe that was in EJ's bedroom. They were hoping to find something inside that would add to the list of charges that they already had pending.

Unbeknownst to Agent Kaplin, Detective Harris had sent a crew over to the house on 56th Street that his informant had told him about a half hour before the raid. He didn't have time to get a warrant so he just went with his gut feeling and sent them in.

To his surprise, they had hit the jackpot. They found an arsenal in the basement along with computer equipment, blank check paper, blank license, credit card material, and the list never ends.

He knew what he had done was illegal, but he hoped to get a plea before they ever found out about it.

Chapter 30

EJ, Ed, and Wan had been in CFCF for two weeks now. They had let Tamara and Yahnise go because they didn't have anything to hold them on. Everybody else was charged with everything from gun possession to fraud by access device.

Shannon and Tiffany were at Riverview Woman's Correctional Facility and they had been charged with everything except gun possession. The judge had set all of their bails at one million dollars cash because of the security of the case.

EJ was sitting in his cell thinking about everything that had just went wrong. He was even wondering what all they had because nobody would tell him anything. Not even his own lawyer had all the details yet.

What he did know was that the mole or what everybody else calls it, the snitch, was still out there running around as if everything was cool. It pissed him off that the judge had given him a one million dollar cash bail. He knew he couldn't put that type of money up without the Feds really running down on him. His wife was at home stressing and he missed the hell out of his son.

As EJ was sitting there thinking about all types of shit, his cell mate came in. "What up nigga? You not going to come work out with us?" Scrap said. Scrap was from Delaware. He came out to Philly trying to get some money with some of his niggas and ended up in a shootout that left a little kid in critical condition. They charged him with attempted murder even though the bullet was meant for someone else.

"Naw, I'm about to get on the Jack (phone) and call my wife. She should be coming up here tomorrow," EJ said, putting his sneakers on.

"Alright, well after that, come out in the yard so we can beat up on Ed and his celi (cell mate) in some basketball," Scrap said, exiting the cell.

They had sent Ed to A23 so that he and EJ wouldn't be on the same block, but Ed was already fucking one of the female guards named Ms. Thomas when he was out on the streets so she got him moved to A21 with EJ. Wan was still in the infirmary nursing his injuries he received from the police beat down.

EJ was heading to the phone when the Correctional Officer (CO) stopped him and told him that his lawyer was here to see him. "Hurry up because he has already been here for thirty minutes," the male CO said.

"Damn and you are just now informing me of this," EJ said as he went to grab his Department of Corrections (DOC) shirt.

"I just got the phone call, smart ass," the CO said with an attitude.

EJ grabbed his pass and went to see what his lawyer was saying. He walked down the hall to the official visiting area. He didn't have to change into a carrot suit (orange jumper) because he didn't have a regular visit.

"Johnson, you are in room four," the visit CO said.

EJ walked into the room, and was immediately greeted by Savino. "Hey man, sorry to be seeing you under these circumstances, but we have some important shit to talk about," he said shaking EJ's hand before both men sat down.

EJ looked at his attorney and said, "Okay, give it to me straight and don't hold anything back."

Savino opened up his briefcase, took some papers out, and sat them on the table. He flipped through the papers and once he found the one he was looking for, he said, "Y'all are in some tight shit right now. They had an informant in your circle the whole damn time filling them in on everything. They wanted to charge you under the Rico Act, but because they let the state handle it, you're being charged with racketeering among other charges."

"So who is this snitch that's trying to put me under the jail," EJ asked Savino.

"I don't have that information yet, but I'm working on it," Savino said in a calm manner.

"How long will I have to sit in here before you will have that information for me?" EJ asked, sounding impatient.

"Maybe a month or two. It could be longer. That's why I'm trying to get you and the rest of your people another bail hearing soon. My whole firm is working on y'all case," Savino said.

"Fuck! I can't be in here that long, man. You have to try to do something to get me out of here," EJ said, pissed off.

"You know I'm on it, so don't worry. As soon as I get that statement, I'll give you the name of the mole," Savino said, taking out a pad and pen.

"No, I don't want that shit. What I want you to do is give it to my worker, Tuck. He'll know what to do from there. Tell him to take care of that ASAP and then he can send it to me," EJ said.

"Okay, but I don't want anything to go wrong with me trying to get you out of here. Without the testimony of the informant, the case will be weak," he said.

EJ was thinking, *"That's what I wanted to hear."*

"Okay, let's get down to business. Tell me everything that happened from the time they first arrived at your house," Savino said ready to take notes.

* * * *

Ed was about to go take a shower so he could get ready for his visit with Tamara. He had his shower shoes in his hand along with his towel and soap. In CFCF, you had to wear your shoes when you took a shower because you never knew when someone would try you.

As he walked towards the shower, he noticed a nigga by the name of Rock that owed him money sitting in his cell. The whole time Ed never knew the dude was on his tier. He made a mental note that he would be getting at him later on that night. Right now, it was time to get ready for his wifey.

* * * *

EJ, Ed, Tamara, Yahnise, and Ziaire were all sitting in the visiting room chatting about everything that was going on. Everybody was giving different opinions about what would happen except for EJ. He was busy playing with his son. You could tell that he missed his family from his body expressions.

"Baby are you okay?" Yahnise asked. Sensing something was wrong.

"Yeah, I was just thinking about some things. It's not that important though. How's everything at home?" he said changing the subject.

"It's good. We miss you though," she said, sounding very sad.

"Don't worry, this will be over soon, and I'll be back home," he said, not giving up hope.

"I understand baby," Yahnise said, rubbing his back for comfort.

EJ and Ed kicked it with their wives for the remainder of their visit. It made the women feel good to see their men. They wished that they were leaving with them.

After the visit, the men headed to the back to get strip searched then they went back to the block. When they got back, a couple of niggas wanted to play Spades for some money. "Come on y'all, we are ready," Ace said, sitting down at the table.

"Hold up, damn! We just got back from the dance floor (visiting room). Can we put our shit up?" Ed said as he headed for his room.

"Don't be in such a rush to get your shit taken, nigga!" EJ said, laughing at Ace and his partner.

They played cards all evening until around 10:00 that night. Ed looked over to EJ and said, "You ready to handle that clown now?"

"Yeah, let's do it while there ain't too many people around," EJ said pulling his banger (jail made knife) out of his waist.

Ace and Wiz saw what was about to go down and said, "I'll drop your twenty dollars in commissary off at your cell." They got up and left so they wouldn't get caught up in the drama that was about to unfold.

Rock had just got out of the shower, not paying attention as EJ and Ed entering. He looked up and his whole body went numb.

"I told you that I was gonna get you," Ed said as he hit him in the neck with the banger, causing blood to shoot out of his neck like a faucet.

EJ moved in and hit him in his chest twice which made him bend over in pain. Then they both started stabbing him repeatedly before taking off their bloody shirts and walking out of his cell. They had stabbed him over one hundred times.

The CO never even noticed anything because she was too busy listening to her music.

They went in their cells and flushed the bloody clothes down the toilet. Then they washed up in the sink.

The CO called count ten minutes later. As she was walking around doing count, she noticed all the blood and the lifeless body. She immediately called for backup.

By the time medical got there, it was too late. They put the jail on lock down to do an investigation.

Ed and EJ weren't worried because they knew they weren't going to get caught. Nobody wasn't going to say anything or else the same thing would happen to them.

* * * *

Two months had went by, but it only seemed like two weeks. EJ was on the phone with his lawyer. He finally got the news he was waiting for.

"They are sending me the affidavit now and the statement with the witness name on it. Since its Friday, you won't be able to get it until Tuesday or Wednesday. I will send it to your friend by e-mail as soon as I get it," Savino said.

"Okay, thanks man, but take it to him and give it to him in person. I will give you the number to call him so you can meet up with him," EJ said so he didn't incriminate himself. He wasn't worried about saying anything over the phone because he was using a cell phone that he had paid a CO five hundred dollars to bring in. He wouldn't say his man's name because he didn't want his lawyer to say it on the phone.

After he gave his lawyer the number, he hung up and let his cell call the party line as he always did around this time.

He sat on his bed and wondered whom the person was that had been bringing his operation down the whole time by running his mouth.

* * * *

Ed had been placed in solitary confinement because two weeks after the stabbing incident, they found a banger inside his mattress. He received ninety days in the hole for that.

Ed didn't care about being in the hole. His focus was on trying to beat this case. He knew that with a state's witness out there roaming free, they didn't have a chance. He just hoped that his friend would take care of everything.

CHAPTER 31

Saturday night was cold as hell as everybody stayed in the house from the snow. The roads closed due to a state of emergency warning that was broadcast over all of the TV and radio stations.

Tuck was sitting in his car with the heat on full blast, waiting for the perfect time to holler at the female he was waiting for. He had just smoked two Dutches of Sour Diesel so he was in full go mode.

After waiting for about an hour, the lights finally went out in the house he was watching. It was now 2:30 a.m. and he wanted to hurry up and get back home to his warm bed.

He took out his Glock and put the silencer on it. Then he tucked it back in his waist. Tuck got out the car and pulled the skully down over his head, and then pulled his hood over his head.

He went across the street and cut through the alley heading towards the back door of the female's crib. He climbed the fence and jimmied the window. Then he slid into the house. Once he was inside, he took his gun out and took the safety off. He started for the stairs when he noticed someone laying on the couch.

Tuck walked up to the sleeping female and aimed his gun at her head. POP! POP! POP!

Tuck put three rounds in her head. He proceeded up the stairs towards the bedrooms. He checked the first room and it was empty.

Then he walked to the second bedroom and that one was empty too. When Tuck reached the master bedroom, he saw a figure laying on top of the comforter. She wasn't wearing anything, but a pair of black thongs. Her body was so beautiful that he almost had second thoughts about the whole situation. He knew what he came to do so he was going to get it done.

He walked over to the bed and stared at the figure before him. He leaned over and smelled her Victoria Secret perfume. It gave him an instant erection. Tuck took his finer and placed it between her legs feeling the heat coming from her pussy. He knew he was wrong, but he just had to have a taste before he killed his victim.

As Tuck went to move his finger, the woman's eyes opened causing him to panic a little. He aimed his gun at her while placing his other hand over her mouth.

"Shhhh. Don't fucking say a word or I will fucking kill you," he said to the woman. "Do you understand?"

She looked at him scared to death and shook her head yes.

Tuck then took his gun and placed it between her legs rubbing her pussy through her thong.

"Open your legs up wide," he said still rubbing her pussy.

She was so scared that she did as she was told. He took the gun and pulled her thong to the side before shoving the gun inside of her.

She tried to scream from the pain, but he still had his hand over her mouth. Looking at her in so much pain gave him a rush of adrenaline.

He didn't want to play anymore so he pulled the trigger while the gun was still inside of her.

POP! POP! POP! POP!

The shots killed her instantly, but he wasn't done yet.

Tuck took his hunting knife out of the case that was connected to his belt, leaned over the dead corpse, and cut her throat. Next, he pulled her tongue through her neck giving her a Columbian necktie. "That's what we do for rats, you fucking Puta," he said as he headed out the room.

Tuck left out of the house the same way he came in. Once he was back in his car, he took the gloves he was wearing and put them in a bag. He looked over to the house and said, "That should teach all you fucking snitches a lesson," before starting his car and leaving the crime scene.

* * * *

Monday afternoon EJ was sitting in his cell listening to his Walkman when he heard the CO walking around passing out mail. When she approached his cell, she said, "Johnson and Reed you both have mail." She passed EJ and his celi their mail. EJ saw the cover of the newspaper, but didn't pay it any attention. He looked at the letter from his lawyer and opened it up.

When EJ read the contents of the letter, his heart felt like it dropped out of his chest. He couldn't believe what he was reading. It took him a minute to re-read the letter. After reading it over, it confirmed what he read the first time.

Then all of a sudden, reality hit him. He dropped the letter and anxiously picked up the newspaper back up and read the article on the front page. That's as far as he could go before tears started flowing down his face like a waterfall.

"Oh my God! What have I done," he said as he covered his face.

EJ's celi jumped off the bed to see what was wrong. "What happened?" he questioned grabbing the paper and reading the front page. The headline said, "Two female bodies were found in a Southwest Philly house yesterday morning shot multiple times."

Scrap looked at his celi and said, "E, what's going on? Do you know them?"

EJ just looked up at his celi and shook his head as the tears continued to flow.

– THE END –

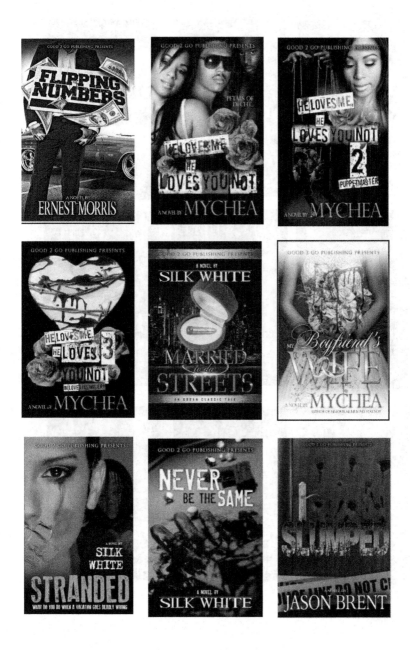

GOOD 2 GO FILMS

Name: _____

Address: _____

City: _____ State: _____ Zip Code: _____

Phone: _____

Email: _____

Method of Payment: ☐ Check ☐ VISA ☐ MASTERCARD

Credit Card#: _____

Name as it appears on card: _____

Signature: _____

Item Name	Price	Qty	Amount
Flipping Numbers	$14.99		
He Loves Me, He Loves You Not - Mychea	$14.99		
He Loves Me, He Loves You Not 2 - Mychea	$14.99		
He Loves Me, He Loves You Not 3 - Mychea	$14.99		
Married To Da Streets – Silk White	$14.99		
My Boyfriend's Wife - Mychea	$14.99		
Never Be The Same – Silk White	$14.99		
Stranded – Silk White	$14.99		
Slumped – Jason Brent	$14.99		
Tears of a Hustler - Silk White	$14.99		
Tears of a Hustler 2 - Silk White	$14.99		
Tears of a Hustler 3 - Silk White	$14.99		
Tears of a Hustler 4- Silk White	$14.99		
Tears of a Hustler 5 – Silk White	$14.99		
Tears of a Hustler 6 – Silk White	$14.99		
The Panty Ripper - Reality Way	$14.99		
The Teflon Queen – Silk White	$14.99		
The Teflon Queen 2 – Silk White	$14.99		
The Teflon Queen – 3 – Silk White	$14.99		
The Teflon Queen – 4 – Silk White	$14.99		
Time Is Money - Silk White	$14.99		
Young Goonz – Reality Way	$14.99		
Subtotal:			
Tax:			
Shipping (Free) U.S. Media Mail:			
Total:			

Make Checks Payable To:
Good2Go Publishing
7311 W Glass Lane
Laveen, AZ 85339

CPSIA information can be obtained at www.ICGtesting.com
Printed in the USA
LVOW04s2131130215

427030LV00012B/140/P